# Claudia and the Sad Good-bye

**Look for these and other books
in the Baby-sitters Club series:**

# Claudia and the Sad Good-bye

## Ann M. Martin

AN
**APPLE**
PAPERBACK

SCHOLASTIC INC.
New York Toronto London Auckland Sydney

Cover art by Hodges Soileau

ISBN 0-590-42503-X

12 11 10 9 8 7 6 5 4 3 2 1          9/8 0 1 2 3 4/9

Printed in the U.S.A.                    28

First Scholastic printing, August 1989

*This book is for
Margaret Martin Vinsel
With Love*

# CHAPTER 1

"Mimi! I'm home! I'm home, Mimi!"

"Hello, my Claudia."

My grandmother greeted me at the door when I got home from school. She kissed my forehead and smiled crookedly at me. Mimi is one of my favorite people. She is a second mother to me.

I dropped my book bag and gym shoes on the floor in the hall. Mom or Dad or even my big sister, Janine, would have looked from my stuff to the stairs, as a silent reminder to take the things up to my bedroom instead of leaving them lying around. If that had happened, I would have left the things for ten minutes or so before I took them to my room, to show my family that they can't all boss me around just because I'm the youngest and not a very good student.

But Mimi didn't say anything about dropping my school stuff on the floor. She didn't even look at it. So I immediately picked it up and ran to my room. When I came downstairs again, I found Mimi in the kitchen, fiddling with cups and a tin of tea leaves.

"Special tea, my Claudia?" she asked me.

"Oh, *yes!*" The day was perfect for special tea. For one thing, it was raining. Outside the window there was nothing but drizzle and dreariness, which I don't mind at all. I love mysteries — and drizzle and dreariness are a good backdrop for any mystery. Also, I didn't have any after-school activities planned. Usually I have a baby-sitting job or an art class, but that afternoon I was free. Most important, special tea with Mimi is wonderful any time.

What is special tea? Special tea is when my grandmother prepares Japanese tea and serves it in cups with no handles that she brought with her when she moved from Japan to America. Then she and I sip the tea and talk, just the two of us.

Mimi likes to prepare special tea completely by herself, even though this is difficult for her now, since she had a stroke last summer and can't move around as easily as she used to. In fact, she can't use her right hand at all. Speech is difficult for her, too. Plus, she's been just plain forgetful lately, and has said and done some pretty weird things. But this day seemed to be a good one, and special tea went smoothly.

It is usually as soothing as Mimi herself.

"So, my Claudia," Mimi began (and I should tell you that I am the only one Mimi calls *her* someone), "how school was?"

"Oh, okay. I didn't do so well on that math test."

"How not so well?"

"A C-minus?" I answered with a question, as if I weren't *sure* that was the grade I'd gotten. But it was. One point lower and it would have been a D-plus.

"Oh," said Mimi. "Well. Studied. Studied hard. I remember. Next better time." That garbled message meant that Mimi remembered that I had studied hard with the help of my dad and my big sister, Janine, who is a genius, and that no doubt I would do better on my next test.

"Thanks, Mimi," I replied, smiling. "Guess what I *did* get a good grade on. That history composition," I answered for her.

"The one I help?"

"Yup. The one you helped me with."

"What grade?"

"B . . . plus!" I said grandly.

Mimi beamed. She had given me the idea to write a composition on a period in Japanese history, but she had really helped only a little. I had done most of the work myself.

I sipped my tea.

I looked at my hands holding my cup, and at Mimi's hands holding her cup. My hands were smooth and creamy-colored and steady. Mimi's were wrinkled and brown like walnuts, and they shook. Mimi is my mother's mother and she's getting pretty old.

As you have probably guessed, Mimi is Japanese. She came to the United States a long time ago, when she was thirty-two. Her husband was Japanese, too, so of course my mom is Japanese. And so is my dad. Janine and I consider ourselves not just Japanese, but Japanese-American, meaning that we're full-blooded Asian but we've lived all our lives in the U.S. Actually, we've lived all our lives here in Stoneybrook, Connecticut. And Mimi has lived all of *my* life in Stoneybrook, because her husband died after Mom and Dad got married, so she moved in with them. Both of my parents were working. They were doing different things then, but now Dad is a partner in an investment firm in Stamford, Connecticut, which is nearby, and Mom is the head librarian at our public library. Anyway, when my grandfather died, Janine the genius had just been born, so Mimi's moving in seemed like the perfect arrangement. My parents could work, and Mimi could help with the house, watch Janine, and not miss her husband quite so much. Three years later, I was born, and there was Mimi to help raise me. Mimi is my friend and the person who understands me the best in the world, even better than my friends.

I smiled at Mimi over our tea cups and she set hers shakily on the table. "No more talking of school," she said. "Tell me art. Sitting for babies." (She meant baby-sitting.)

So we talked about my art and baby-sitting. And I poured the tea when Mimi's hands shook too much, and helped her with words she couldn't remember.

At last Mimi said, "I start dinner. Now. What do you?"

"I think I'll go upstairs and work on my painting."

Mimi nodded. I left her in the kitchen and went to my room.

I hate school. But here is what I love: reading mysteries, especially Nancy Drews; baby-sitting; art. Not only do I love art, I'm good at it. Really good at it. And thank heavens for that. I better be good at something since Janine is so smart in school. How smart is she? She's smart enough to be a high school junior who takes courses at a college in Stoneybrook. That's right, a *college*. When I say she's a genius, I mean it. Her I.Q. is, like, nine million or something. We used to sort of hate each other, but as we grow up, we get along much better. For one thing, we've been worried about Mimi a lot lately, and that's brought us closer together. Worry and fear can do that.

I looked around my messy room. My room is only messy because I have to keep so many art materials stored in it. I like painting, drawing, pottery, sculpture, crafts, and more. So I've got an easel and paints and charcoals, and boxes and boxes of stuff *everywhere*. My current project is a painting. I'm trying something new. I think of it as "stop-action." Imagine that you're watching a movie on a VCR — a movie with a lot of action — and in the middle of a really exciting scene, you press the pause button. That's how I wanted this picture to look — as if time had halted and people had been stopped with spoons halfway to their mouths, or a dropped object in midair, or a bird about to land on a branch, its feet just inches above it, its wings still outstretched.

I paused in my painting and looked out the window and across the street. I could see Mary Anne's house clearly. Mary Anne Spier is one of a group of my friends who have formed a business called the Baby-sitters Club. I'm the vice-president of the club. Mary Anne is the secretary, and our president is Kristy Thomas. Besides us, there are three other members, plus two associate members (I'll explain about them in a minute), and one member in New York City. (I'll explain about her, too.)

Our club meets three afternoons a week, and although our members are very, *very* different people, we get along well. We're like the pieces of a jigsaw puzzle. Put us all together and we make a great picture.

Let me tell you about my friends, beginning with Kristy, since she's the president. Kristy started the club herself. It was her idea. That's an important thing about Kristy. She's full of ideas. She's also outgoing, sort of bossy, a tomboy, and has a big mouth. Okay, a huge mouth. She's thirteen and in eighth grade, like me and most of the club members. She doesn't care much about clothes or makeup yet. *Some-times, she'll put on a little mascara, but that's it. And she always wears the same kind of outfit: jeans, a turtleneck, a sweater, and running shoes. Kristy has brown hair (longish), brown eyes, and is the shortest kid in our class. Her family is pretty unusual. Her mom and dad got divorced a long time ago. She has three brothers — two big ones in high school, and David Michael, who is seven. Then her mom married this millionaire (no joke). Watson has two little kids of his own, Karen, who's six, and Andrew, who's four. *And* recently her family adopted Emily Michelle, a two-year-old Vietnamese girl. Then there's Kristy's Nannie, her grandma, who's really neat and decided to move in with them and help care for Emily. The whole family lives in Watson's mansion on the other side of Stoneybrook. (Well, Karen and Andrew only live there every other weekend and for two weeks during the summer. The rest of the time they live with their mom and stepfather, not too far away.)

As I mentioned before, I'm the vice-president of the club. You already know a lot about me, except for a few things. I'm addicted to junk food. Mom and Dad don't really like me to have it, so I have to buy it secretly and hide it around my room. It's everywhere. Despite all the junk I eat, my complexion is pretty nice. Smooth. My friends are always saying I'm so lucky because I don't get pimples. Here's what I look like besides my complexion: dark, almond-shaped eyes and long, *long* silky, black hair that I wear all different ways. And I dress on the wild side. Kristy's outfits and mine are like night and day. Here's an example: At the moment I'm wearing lavender plaid cuffed pants with suspenders over a green shirt with buttons down the front, a matching lavender beret (and *not* just because I'm at my easel), and fleece-lined, high-top sneakers which I must admit are uncomfortably hot, but they *look great.* Also, I've got on earrings shaped like Christmas tree lights that actually blink on and off. I'm not sure why I chose to wear them, since it's nowhere near Christmas, but I love jewelry, like to make my own sometimes, and have pierced ears. (Kristy doesn't. Doesn't have pierced ears, that is.) But I have three — two holes in one ear, and one in the other.

Our club secretary is Mary Anne, who lives across the street. Kristy is one of her best friends. They used to live next door to each other, until Kristy's family moved to Watson's house. Mary Anne is not much like Kristy at all. They sort of illustrate the saying about opposites attracting. Mary Anne is shy and reserved. She's very romantic, cries easily, and hates sports. She's also the only one of *any* of us club members to have a steady boyfriend. His name is Logan Bruno, and he's one of the associate members of the Baby-sitters Club. Mary Anne and Kristy *do* look a little alike, though. Mary Anne also has brown hair and eyes and is on the short side. She used to dress kind of like Kristy, too, but lately her outfits have become trendier. However, Mary Anne doesn't have, and never will have, pierced ears. Mary Anne's family is the smallest of any of the club members. It's just her and her dad. Mrs. Spier died a long time ago. Mary Anne has no brothers or sisters, but she does have a gray kitten named Tigger.

Dawn Schafer is the treasurer of our club. Dawn moved to Stoneybrook with her mother and younger brother, Jeff, about a year ago when her parents got divorced. Mrs. Schafer chose Stoneybrook because she grew up here and her parents still live here, but the move was a shock to Dawn and Jeff since *they* grew up in California. In fact, it was so much of a shock to Jeff that eventually he moved back to California to live with his dad. So now half of

Dawn's family lives here, and the other half lives three thousand miles away. Thank goodness Dawn's grandparents are in Stoneybrook. Dawn is the most independent person I know. She's reliable and responsible and organized, but she does things her own way. She never gets swayed by what anyone (or everyone) else is doing. She has her own style of dress, which we call California casual, and she sticks to a total health-food diet, even though some of the kids at school tease her about the weird stuff she eats, and the fact that she won't touch candy or junk food. Dawn lives in an old farmhouse with a secret passage (and maybe a ghost) in it, she has the longest, blondest hair and the bluest eyes I've ever seen, and she's Mary Anne's other best friend. (Her mom and Mr. Spier go out on dates sometimes!)

Our club has two junior officers, Jessi Ramsey and Mallory Pike. While the rest of us are in eighth grade, Jessi and Mal are eleven and in sixth grade. That's why they're junior officers. They're only allowed to baby-sit after school or on weekends; not at night unless they're sitting for their own brothers and sisters. Jessi and Mal are best friends. Like Kristy and Mary Anne, they're similar in some ways and different in some ways. The biggest difference is that Jessi is black and Mallory is white. Also, Jessi has just one younger sister and brother, and Mal has *seven* younger sisters and brothers — and three of the boys are identical triplets! Both girls like to read, especially horse stories, and both feel that their parents aren't letting them grow up fast enough. But Mal loves to write and draw and might want to become a children's book author, while Jessi is a talented, and I mean *talented*, ballet dancer. They're really neat, even if they are a little less mature than the rest of us club members.

Our associate officers are Shannon Kilbourne and Logan Bruno. They don't come to our meetings and no one except Kristy knows Shannon very well because she lives way across town in Kristy's ritzy neighborhood, and doesn't go to Stoneybrook Middle School with the rest of us. We do know Logan, though, and if you were to ask Mary Anne to describe him, all she'd say is, "Incredible." She would mean good-looking, nice, thoughtful, funny, etc., and he is those things. I like him a lot, but no one knows him better than Mary Anne does.

There's one other person I feel I should tell you about. She's only sort of a club member, but she *is* my best friend. Her name is Stacey McGill, and she lived in Stoneybrook for just about one year. She and her parents had lived in New York City, then her dad's company transferred him here, then, after one year, back to New York. Weird, huh? But it was lucky for me, because if none of that had happened, I'd never have met my first and only best friend. Stacey was a club member, of course. And she and I are *so* much alike. We couldn't look more different, but we both love wild clothes and I guess we're a little boy-crazy. Stacey has diabetes, which is a huge drag, but she copes with it pretty well. Now that she's back in New York, she calls herself the New York branch of the Baby-sitters Club, but it isn't the same, and I miss her a *lot*.

I stopped staring out the window and day-dreaming about the Baby-sitters Club and my friends, and went back to work on my painting again. A few minutes later, Mimi came into my room. For someone with a limp, she manages the stairs pretty well — but only sometimes. Other times, they frighten her.

My grandmother stood behind me and studied the painting.

"A beautiful," she said at last.

"Thanks, Mimi," I replied.

Mimi put her arm around me. "Start dinner?" she asked.

Hadn't she started an hour ago? I wondered. But all I said was, "Do you want me to give you a hand?" (I'm used to Mimi's forgetfulness.)

Mimi nodded.

Arm in arm, we walked slowly to the top of the stairs. We walked even more slowly down them. When we reached the kitchen Mimi discovered that she'd forgotten what she'd planned for dinner, so I helped her start over.

Mimi needs lots of help these days.

It's a little bit hard on our family.

# CHAPTER 2

"Claudia, Claudia!" called an urgent voice, and Mallory Pike burst into my bedroom. She looked close to tears. It was a Wednesday afternoon, just ten minutes before the beginning of a meeting of the Baby-sitters Club. "Mimi just scolded me and told me never to take her shopping again because we have to wait too long to get into the dressing rooms. She sounded really mad at me." (All my friends call my grandmother Mimi. That's what she likes.)

"Sit down," I said, leading Mallory to my bed. "I guess Mimi never yelled at you before, did she?"

"Well," said Mal shakily, "she wasn't exactly yelling, but — "

"I know what you mean." I plopped down next to Mal.

"Anyway, no, she never talked to me that

15

way before — and I never took her shopping. When would I have taken her shopping? And why would she think *I'd* take her shopping instead of you or Janine or one of your parents?"

Before I could answer, Mal rushed on. "And then she seemed like her old self again. Her voice went back to normal, and she pulled *this* out of her pocket and gave it to me." Mallory opened her hand and showed me a small china bird that had been part of Mimi's bird collection for as long as I could remember. "Mimi said she's known me since I was little and she really wants me to have this. . . . You don't mind, do you? I mean, I didn't ask for it or anything."

I did mind a little, but not because Mimi had chosen Mal, not me, to have the bird. I minded because for Mimi this was a new weird behavior that I didn't understand. All I said, though, was, "No, of course not," and Mal smiled and looked like she felt better.

Then Kristy came in, or maybe I should say *blew* in, and Mimi was immediately forgotten.

"Hi, you guys!" cried Kristy. "Are we the only ones here so far?" She checked her watch. "Five minutes till meeting time. Any Oreos, Claud?"

I felt winded just listening to Kristy, but I began a search for this package of Oreos which I was pretty sure was inside my hollow book, one of my best hiding places. The other good hiding places are behind a row of Nancy Drews on my shelf, and in boxes under my bed, labeled things like ART SUPLYS. (I am not the world's greatest speller.)

Maybe I better tell you how our club works, before things get underway. Kristy, Mary Anne, Dawn, Mal, Jessi, and I meet Monday, Wednesday, and Friday afternoons from five thirty until six. We have done a lot of advertising (mostly with fliers and in the newspaper), so people know that these are the times we meet. When they need baby-sitters they call us at those times. We provide the sitters — and get tons of jobs this way.

The club started back at the beginning of seventh grade when Kristy saw how hard it was for her mom to find a sitter for David Michael (who was six then) at a time when neither Kristy nor her older brothers, Sam and Charlie, could watch him. Mrs. Thomas (well, she was Mrs. Thomas then, but now she's Mrs. Watson Brewer) had to make call after call trying to find an available sitter. And Kristy thought to herself, Wouldn't it be great if Mom could make one phone call and find, like, a whole nest of sitters?

That was the beginning of the Baby-sitters Club. She asked Mary Anne, me, and Stacey (who was my new friend then), to join her, and we started advertising to let people know what we were going to do, and when they could reach us. We began receiving calls at our first meeting. We were amazed!

Here's how we run the meetings: officially. As president, Kristy insists on that. She is always a take-charge person, and usually a no-nonsense person. At the beginning of every meeting, she puts a visor on her head, a pencil over one ear, and plunks herself down in my director's chair. (The meetings are held in my room because I have my own phone and my own phone number.) Then she asks Dawn to collect club dues if it's a Monday, and then she just, well, runs things. She makes us keep a club notebook in which each of us is responsible for writing up every job we go on. Once a week, we're supposed to read the past week's entries so that we all know what's happened at the houses where our friends have sat. Plus, we often find good solutions to sitting problems in the notebook. I look at it this way: Kristy deserves to be the president. She's good at being a boss (when she's not actually being *bossy*), she's a natural leader, and besides, the club was her idea.

I'm the vice-president mostly because of my phone. If we held our meetings in anyone else's room we'd have to tie up some adult's phone line three times a week — and get calls for people who aren't club members. Actually, there's a little more to my job than just owning a phone. A lot of times, baby-sitting calls come in while we're not having a meeting. Then I have to take down the information about who needs a sitter when, for how long, and for how many kids, and call my friends to see who's available to take the job.

As secretary, Mary Anne has the most complicated job of all. She's perfect for it, though, because she's organized, precise, and has terribly neat handwriting. What does she do? She keeps our record book up-to-date and in order, and schedules all of our jobs. This includes keeping track of the club members' personal schedules, too — dance lessons, art classes, dentist appointments (or in Mal's case, orthodontist appointments). The record book is the most important feature of our club. It's very official, so of course it was Kristy's idea. Apart from the appointment pages where Mary

Anne does our scheduling, it has pages where she records our clients' names and addresses, the number of children they have, and vital information, such as children who have food allergies or special fears. Also in the record book is space for recording the money we earn, and for keeping track of our treasury. That's Dawn's job, though, so on to Dawn.

Our poor treasurer has the awful job of collecting dues from us club members every week. We hate parting with any of our money, but Dawn (being Dawn) just does her job and isn't bothered by our griping. The money in the treasury is used for several things. First of all, fun stuff — throwing slumber parties or pizza parties from time to time. Our club isn't *all* work. Secondly, to pay Charlie Thomas, Kristy's oldest brother, to drive her to and from meetings now that she lives across town. The third thing we spend the money on is toys for our Kid-Kits. Kid-Kits are boxes that we decorated ourselves (we each have one) and filled with our old games, toys, and books. We take the Kid-Kits with us sometimes when we baby-sit, and the kids love them — which makes *us* popular baby-sitters! Anyway, most of the stuff in the kits, like books and games, never wears out or gets used up. But we do have to replace crayons, activity books, soap bubbles, and things like that. The treasury money is supposed to cover those expenses.

Mallory and Jessi, our junior officers, don't have real duties the way the rest of us do, but they sure help take the pressure off of us. Our club is very successful. We get so many jobs, in fact, that when Stacey (who was our first treasurer — Dawn took over after she left) moved back to New York, we decided to replace her with *two* new club members. It's kind of a pain that Jessi and Mal are too young to sit at night, but at least when they cover more of the afternoon jobs, it frees the rest of us up for the evenings.

Okay, now I'll tell you about Logan Bruno (the love of Mary Anne's life) and Shannon Kilbourne, our two associate club members. They don't come to meetings, but they are good sitters whom we know we can call on if a job comes in that *none* of us is free to take. That might sound unlikely, but it does happen. Just last week, someone needed a sitter on an afternoon when Mallory had an orthodontist appointment, I had an art class, Jessi had a dance rehearsal, and the rest of us were going to be baby-sitting. Whew! Shannon took that job, thank goodness.

Anyway, after some searching around my room on that Wednesday afternoon, I found a new package of Double Stuf Oreos and handed them to Kristy in the director's chair. While she was opening them, Jessi, Dawn, and Mary Anne came in. Mallory moved off the bed to sit on the floor with Jessi, while Mary Anne and Dawn and I settled ourselves in a row on my bed. These are our usual spots for club meetings.

No sooner had Kristy asked if anyone had club business to discuss, than the phone rang.

"I'll get it!" exclaimed Kristy. "First call of the meeting!" Kristy picked up the phone. "Hello, Baby-sitters Club. . . . Yes? . . . Yes?" She sounded puzzled. Then she handed the phone to me and said, cupping her hand over the receiver, "It's Mrs. Addison. Remember her? And she wants to talk to you."

This was not standard club procedure. Usually, whoever answers the phone (and it isn't always Kristy), takes down the information about the job, and then hangs up to give Mary Anne a chance to study our schedule. When we've found someone who's available for the job, we call the client back to tell him or her who the sitter will be.

But our club had baby-sat for the Addison

kids only a couple of times, so maybe Mrs. Addison had forgotten the procedure.

I took the phone from Kristy, feeling curious. "Hi, Mrs. Addison?" I said. Then I listened to her for a long time. When I hung up the phone, I turned to the other girls and said, "Guess what? She doesn't want a baby-sitter, she wants an art teacher."

"Huh?" said Kristy.

"Oh, don't tell me. For Corrie. Or Sean. Right?" spoke up Dawn, who's the only one of us who has sat for the Addisons.

"Yeah, for Corrie," I replied. "How did you know?"

"Because all Mr. and Mrs. Addison want is time for themselves, so they shuttle poor Corrie and Sean from class to class on weekends and after school. Corrie's only nine, and Sean is ten, and I bet they've both already taken basketball, dance, drama, creative writing, football, baseball, and anything else the Addisons can think of."

"Well, now Mrs. Addison's thought of art, and she knows that I'm pretty good at art *and* that I like kids, so she's wondering if I'd give Corrie an art lesson once a week. I guess that would be sort of like a baby-sitting job. . . . Wouldn't it?"

"Sure," replied Kristy. "You'd have to charge more than usual because you'd need to provide materials, but I don't see why — "

"Hey!" I cried, interrupting Kristy. I couldn't help it. For once, *I'd* had a great idea. "Maybe I could start a little art class. Like on Saturdays in our basement. Gabbie and Myriah Perkins love art projects. So does Jamie Newton. That would be fun. And good experience for me, in case I ever want to be an art teacher."

"And," said Kristy slowly, "it would show people that our club can do more than just baby-sit. I think it would be good for business."

"I'd need some help, though," I said slowly. "I don't know if I could manage a class alone."

"If you hold the class on Saturdays, I could help you," spoke up Mary Anne. "We'll split the money sixty-forty, since you'll be in charge."

It seemed like a great arrangement. If Mrs. Addison agreed, then all systems would be go.

Mrs. Addison did agree. The meeting ended on a happy note.

# CHAPTER 3

Sometimes when my friends leave after a club meeting, I feel a little let down. Suddenly my room is quiet again. And it's funny, but that's when I miss Stacey the most. Knowing that my only *best* friend is all the way in New York City makes me feel bad — but just for a few moments. Then I remember that Mimi is home and I can run downstairs and help her fix dinner.

That was just what I did after the meeting when Mary Anne and I decided to hold art classes. Only lately I haven't been just helping Mimi fix dinner, I've pretty much been doing it for her, or at least directing her, if she insists on doing things herself. She's just not too trustworthy in the kitchen anymore. Her hands shake, so I worry when she's using knives or the vegetable peeler. And (I know this is gross, but it's true) she's not very sanitary anymore, either. She's always forgetting to wash her hands before she begins cooking. She doesn't remember to wash food either, like raw chicken pieces or lettuce. And I'm afraid she's going to give us all food poisoning sometime by thawing out a piece of meat, deciding not to serve it after all, and then refreezing it without cooking it first. That's a wonderful way to get salmonella. Plus I worry about matches, the stove, the oven, you name it. Of course, I only need to worry on her bad days. On her good days, no problem. Which is why my parents haven't banned Mimi from the kitchen yet. They know it would take away her sense of usefulness and independence — and that on the bad days, I'll cook or supervise.

"Mimi!" I exclaimed as I entered the kitchen. "I've got a good idea! Let's have a fancy candlelight dinner tonight. You set the table in the dining room with our good china and put out candles and everything."

"Yes. Fine," replied Mimi vaguely.

I was glad she agreed to that. After the business with Mallory that afternoon, I could tell she was having a bad time, and I wanted to make the dinner myself.

During the next hour, my parents came

home from their jobs, and Janine returned from her college course called Advances and Trends in Computerized Biopsychiatry. (Or something like that. I don't know the meaning of any of those words except "and" and "in.")

Everyone was surprised and pleased by our formal dinner. Mimi and I exchanged a secret smile as Mom exclaimed, "Oh, how lovely!" and Janine cried, "Candlelight!" and Dad said, "Chicken and rice, my favorite." (So it wasn't fancy food. At least the meal *looked* fancy.)

My family took our usual places at the table.

I said grandly, "I will serve the first course."

"First course!" repeated Dad.

"Yup," I replied, and then added casually as I was walking around the table with the soup tureen, "By the way, I got a B-plus on my history composition." (I failed to say anything about the math test.)

"Gosh," said Janine, and I couldn't tell whether she was more impressed by the grade or the pea soup, which she was looking at through her thick, round glasses.

I served Mom, then stepped over to Mimi (whom I probably should have served first, but oh, well). Just as I was dipping the ladle into the tureen, Mimi kind of slithered down in her chair.

"Mimi?" I said, hastily setting the hot tureen on the table where it left a mark that we've never been able to get off.

"Do not . . . do not . . . no feel well." Mimi slumped sideways and Dad and Mom both jumped out of their chairs. Dad caught Mimi just before she hit the floor.

"Call the paramedics, Claudia," said Mom in a tone you don't ignore.

I didn't even look back at Mimi. I just raced for the kitchen phone and made the call. The paramedics reached our house in ten minutes. I was waiting outside for them and led them into the dining room, where Mom and Dad had laid Mimi on the floor and covered her with a blanket.

"Is she dead?" I whispered to Janine, who was hovering nearby, not knowing what to do.

"No," replied my sister, sounding surprised. "Listen."

I tried to, over the commotion of the paramedics and their equipment. Mimi wasn't dead. She wasn't even unconscious. She was *talking*. But she was all confused. I heard her mention everything from "the old country" to shopping with Mallory. Sometimes her eyes were closed, sometimes open. She was disoriented and probably embarrassed.

"Low blood pressure," I heard one technician say. Then, "Semiconscious. Doesn't know where she is."

A few minutes later the ambulance drove off with Mimi in it. Mom rode with her. Dad and Janine and I followed them in our car. Nobody said a word on the way to the hospital.

What happened next is pretty boring, so I won't even go into it. All you need to know is that Mimi was admitted to a hospital room (it seemed to take a long time), but since she no longer acted too sick, we just stayed with her until she fell asleep, and then we went home. Before we did that, one doctor did give her a shot of something after he examined her briefly, but he didn't hook her up to any machines and no one was rushing around wringing their hands or calling, "Code blue!" So even with Mimi in the hospital, I felt relieved.

Janine and I even went to school the next morning, and Dad went to his office, but Mom took a personal day off from work to be with Mimi at the hospital. And, of course, I went straight to the hospital from school that afternoon. I'd had a baby-sitting job lined up, but

Mallory was able to take it over for me.

I peeked into Mimi's private room, carrying a small teddy bear behind my back that I'd bought at the hospital gift shop. I figured everyone would be sending Mimi flowers, and that flowers are nice to look at, but that she might want something to hug, especially when she was getting a shot, so I bought the bear.

I tiptoed into the room because Mom had her finger to her lips, signaling to me that Mimi was asleep. I nodded. Then I set the bear on her bed, and Mom and I silently left the room.

Out in the hallway, Mom kissed me and smiled. "How was school?" she asked.

"Fine," I replied. "How's Mimi? What's wrong with her?"

Mom shook her head. "The doctors aren't sure. She had some tests today and they think it's a problem with her blood, but they don't know just what."

"Leukemia?" I whispered, terrified.

"No," said Mom. "And not plain old anemia, either."

"Hemophilia?"

My mother smiled. "You have to be born with that."

"Oh." I paused. "You know, if you want to

30

go to work for awhile, you can. Mallory took my baby-sitting job for me. I can stay with Mimi for the rest of the afternoon."

"We-ell . . ." After some hemming and hawing (Mom's term), she took me up on my offer.

So I spent the afternoon with Mimi.

She slept. I held her hand.

Two more days went by. No one could figure out what was wrong with Mimi's blood. They did test after test, and Mimi talked about weirder and weirder things. They even tested her for something called toxoplasmosis, which you get mainly from cats. I told this one doctor that we've never had a cat, but he didn't care.

I spent the afternoons at the hospital with Mimi, since my family all thought *my* activities were less important than *theirs*. I didn't mind much, though. I guess. And I was pleased to be the one who was at Mimi's side when the doctors, as a last resort, decided to give her a couple of pints of fresh, healthy blood. Boy, did that do the trick! Soon we had a new Mimi on our hands, one who wasn't dizzy or faint, whose appetite came back, and who started talking like a normal person again.

The next day they gave her some more blood.

"I think I would take little walk," Mimi said.

"You want to take a walk?" I asked her. (Of course, *I* was the one there that afternoon. I was missing an art class.)

"Not outside. Just in hospital. Okay?" said Mimi.

I checked with a nurse. It was okay. Guess where we walked? To the nursery! We stood outside a big glass window and looked at eight babies in their cribs or isolettes or whatever they're called.

"I see Asian baby," said Mimi, pleased.

"Look at all his hair!" I exclaimed. "Or her hair. It stands straight up."

"You look like that. When baby," Mimi told me.

"No, I didn't!" I cried.

"Yes. Yes." Mimi smiled fondly at the memory. She squeezed my hand, and I felt bad for even *thinking* about missing art classes and stuff.

The next day, Thursday, Mimi went home. She'd been in the hospital for just over a week, and no one had a clue as to what was wrong with her, but she wasn't faint or dizzy or weak. She was her old self. Maybe she was like a car that just needed its oil changed.

Maybe.

But I still thought it was weird not to know what was wrong. I think the doctors thought so, too, because they told Mimi to stay in bed as much as possible for awhile. If she was well, why did she have to stay in bed?

So Mimi was home with us again. She could be on her own for short periods of time, but Mom and Dad took turns staying home with her for part of every day, and guess who got to watch her in the afternoons? Me. Janine had a big biopsychiatry test coming up, and my parents let her study for it all she wanted.

One Wednesday afternoon, Mimi asked for special tea. I fixed it and served it to her in bed.

"No!" cried Mimi. "All wrong!"

"*What* is wrong with it?" I asked testily.

Mimi couldn't find the words to explain.

I grabbed up the tray and huffed out of the room with it.

"Sorry, my Claudia," Mimi called after me in a small voice.

I didn't answer.

On Friday, right before a meeting of the Baby-sitters Club, Mimi asked me to help her to the bathroom. When she was back in bed, she asked for a glass of water. Then, as my friends started to arrive, she said, "Bored. Newspaper?"

It was 5:35. Upstairs, Kristy was waiting for me impatiently. I was sure of it. So I gathered up a stack of magazines and newspapers and threw them on the foot of Mimi's bed.

"Anything else?" I asked rudely.

Mimi's gentle eyes filled with tears. She shook her head.

Of course I felt terrible. But I had to go upstairs to the meeting.

"Mimi, I'm sorry," I told her, and fled from her room.

And I was sorry. Very sorry.

I was also sick and tired of being Mimi's maid.

# CHAPTER 4

I think that Friday, for me, was the lowest point of Mimi's illness.

It had been awful and scary to see her being loaded onto a stretcher in our dining room, or to see her with bags of blood flowing into her arms, but what I did to her that Friday afternoon was unforgivable. I apologized to her three different times after dinner that night, but I felt only a little better.

Luckily, I have learned that sometimes really awful things are followed by really wonderful things. And guess what — Friday was followed by Saturday (duh), which was the day of the first art class that Mary Anne and I gave. And the art class was wonderful!

Here's who had signed up for it: Corrie Addison (of course), Myriah and Gabbie Perkins, Jamie Newton, Marilyn and Carolyn Arnold (twins!), and Matt Braddock, this wonderful little boy whom Jessi sits for a lot who's totally deaf. We love him to bits, but he and the others, put together, made up an odd class. Mary Anne and I would be teaching five girls and two boys, including twins and a deaf child, ranging in age from two and a half (Gabbie) to nine (Corrie).

Mary Anne and I had decided to hold the art classes in my basement. "That makes the most sense," I said. "All my materials are right upstairs in my room. And Mom said we could use that big utility table down there if we spread newspapers over it and under it. And we have those folding chairs the kids can sit on."

"Perfect," agreed Mary Anne. "Plus, your basement is finished. It's carpeted and heated. Ours is just a dark, old, cold basement with a cement floor that leaks when it rains." Mary Anne paused. "What should we do with the kids at their first lesson?"

"Experiment with paper, paint, and water, I think," I replied. "That's something anyone can do. You know, we'll just let Gabbie mess around. The older kids might want to make watercolor scenes on damp paper. Or do other things. I think the class should be fun and relaxed. We shouldn't tell the kids every little thing to do. We'll let them be creative."

Mary Anne nodded. "Okay," she replied.

Our art class was to be held from eleven o'clock to twelve-thirty each Saturday. I was sure, on that first day, that Mary Anne would get nervous and that she would arrive long before anyone else, especially since she lives right across the street.

But Corrie rang our bell first. It was only 10:45. By the time I opened our front door, Mrs. Addison's car was halfway down the driveway.

"You must be Corrie," I said to the little girl standing on our front steps.

She nodded shyly. Corrie was very pretty, with brownish-blonde hair cut straight across her forehead in bangs, and straight around her shoulders below. Her eyes were framed by long, dark lashes. She was small for her age and had no color at all in her cheeks.

She didn't smile, either. Just nodded and stepped inside when I held the door open for her. "Sorry I'm early," she said in a voice so soft I could barely hear it.

"Hey, no problem," I told her. "Listen, I'm Claudia, and I'm going to be one of your teachers. Your other teacher will be Mary Anne. She'll be here soon."

I took Corrie down to the basement. As it turned out, it was a good thing her mother had dropped her off early. By the time Mary Anne and the other kids arrived, Corrie and I had had a chance to talk, she'd chosen a place for herself at the table, and she knew what the day's art project was. She seemed to need to be sure of things in order to feel comfortable.

And so the lesson began. Mary Anne was afraid it would be a mess, but it wasn't. It was just plain fun.

Gabbie Perkins spent most of the morning experimenting with mixing paints in paper cups. She never made a picture. "Look! Look, Claudee Kishi!" she kept exclaiming. "I just made pink!" Or, "I just made . . . made, um . . . a mess." The mess was a greenish-brown color.

Myriah Perkins worked seriously on a picture of Laura, her baby sister, and Matt worked equally seriously at making inkblots. I showed him how to drop paint on one side of a piece of paper, fold it in half, and wind up with symmetrical designs.

"Butterflies," Matt signed to me. (He

doesn't speak. He signs words with his hands.)

Carolyn and Marilyn spent a lot of the lesson trying to fool Jamie Newton. They kept asking him to guess which one of them was which. They weren't dressed alike, and they have different haircuts, but they still look similar; and anyway, Jamie couldn't keep their rhyming names straight.

"You're . . . you're Marilyn," he'd say as Carolyn asked, for the fourteenth time, "Who am I?" Finally he began calling both of them Very Lynn, which they didn't like.

The twins painted identical pictures of just what you'd expect — a house with four windows, a door, a chimney, a curlicue of smoke rising from the chimney, a strip of blue sky across the top of the paper, and a strip of green grass across the bottom of the paper.

Jamie, who is four, used his paints to give a lesson on colors and shapes to Gabbie, who already knows her colors and shapes. She tried to be patient, though.

"You get a J-plus," Jamie told her when, just to make him keep quiet, Gabbie made a red circle for him.

Corrie laughed for the first time since she'd arrived.

All morning I'd been keeping my eye on Corrie's work. She hadn't spoken to the other children, and had worked silently and thoughtfully. She was creating an imaginary landscape and I knew that her work was good — awfully good — for a nine-year-old. So I told her that.

"You know what?" she confided, almost in a whisper. "I like art. I do. I never told Mommy, but I like it. And I don't like ballet or piano lessons or basketball." Awhile later, she asked me (always waiting for me to come peer over her shoulder, never calling to me), "Do you know where my mommy is right now? Do you know what she's doing?"

I shook my head.

"My daddy? Or Sean?"

"Nope. What are they doing?"

"I don't know. Well, Sean is at his tuba lesson, but I don't know about Mommy and Daddy. . . . I wonder why I'm taking art lessons now, too. . . . But I like my painting. . . . When will Mommy be here? I want her to come back."

It was hard to keep up with Corrie. I looked at my watch. "Class is over in five minutes," I announced.

Corrie smiled.

We cleaned up the table.

Mary Anne walked Jamie and the Perkins girls home. Mr. Arnold arrived for the twins, and Haley Braddock, Matt's older sister, walked over to pick him up. Matt signed "butterfly" to me again with a big grin and waved his paper as he trotted off with Haley.

Corrie and I were left waiting on my front steps. We waited and waited. Corrie looked abandoned, like an orphan.

Mrs. Addison finally arrived half an hour late.

Corrie was the only one who took home a dry painting.

# CHAPTER 5

Saturday

Our art classes aren't real baby-sitting jobs, but Claudia and I know full well that we have to write about them in the notebook, don't we, Kristy? So here goes. Today was our second lesson. Claud is so good with the kids and with sensing what they're ready for, art-wise. Last week, she saw what they can and can't do, what they like and dislike, and gave them a chance to experiment in their new class. So today she began a real art project, one the kids will work on for several weeks — — papier-mâché puppets. This should be a messy and fun project.

*Sure enough, the day started out as fun. The kids were really excited about making puppets. And, as you can imagine, Claudia is going to let each one make whatever he or she wants -- from Jamie's outer space monster to Carrie's Nancy Drew. So the lesson got off to a great start, but it ended in tragedy. I know that sounds corny, but it's true....*

I don't know if what Mary Anne wrote is corny — I'm not good at English-class stuff like that — but it sure was true. Every kid who had been at the lesson the week before was back. And when Mary Anne and I told them about the puppets and how to make them, you should have heard the excitement:

"I'm going to make our Cabbage Patch doll," announced Gabbie.

"But why? We already have one," Myriah pointed out. "Caroline Eunice."

"Well, we should have two." Gabbie paused and then said graciously, "You can have the doll for keeps and I'll take the puppet." (The doll is Myriah's anyway.)

"Okay," agreed her sister. "And I'm going to make a rabbit."

"I'm going to make a witch!" said Marilyn Arnold gleefully.

"A space monster . . . grrr!" growled Jamie.

I had a signing session with Matt to make sure he understood what we were doing, and finally he grinned and signed that he was going to make a baseball player.

The ideas flew — except from Corrie, who merely looked thoughtful.

"Corrie?" I said after awhile. "Do you know what you'd like to make?"

"Nancy Drew," she whispered.

"Really? *Nancy Drew?*" I couldn't help exclaiming. "You like Nancy Drew?"

"Yes!" said Corrie, in the most enthusiastic voice I'd ever heard her use. "You like her, too?"

"Sure," I said. "Nancy Drews are my favorite books."

Corrie beamed. And it was then that both Mary Anne and I realized that some sort of bond was growing between Corrie and me. A bond like the one my friend Stacey used to have with Charlotte Johanssen, a kid our club sits for a lot.

So, with the kids' ideas flowing, Mary Anne

44

helped me set out bowls of water, strips of newspaper we'd cut up the evening before, a jar of flour, and a big tin for dipping the strips into the papier-mâché once it was made.

Then we handed each child a balloon.

"Baby balloons," Gabbie noted.

"She means they're not blown up," Myriah interpreted for us.

"What are they for?" asked Carolyn Arnold.

"Those balloons — after we blow them up — will be the puppets' heads. Well, the forms for the heads," I said. "Then we'll cover them with papier-mâché, then — "

"Claudia! My Claudia!" called a voice.

It was Mimi. She was standing at the top of the steps to the basement. What was she doing there? She wasn't even supposed to be out of bed.

"Mimi!" I called back. "Don't try to come down the stairs." Where was the rest of my family? I knew Mom was at the grocery store. But what about Dad and Janine? Why weren't they keeping an eye on Mimi?

"Don't come down," I said again, but it was too late. Mimi was already halfway down the stairs, and not even holding onto the banister. Had she simply forgotten how teetery she could be?

"Why can't she come down?" asked Myriah.

There was no time to answer her question. Mary Anne was dashing up the staircase to Mimi.

It seemed easier to help her the rest of the way down than to try to turn her around and get her back upstairs. So that's what Mary Anne did in her gentle, understanding way. She led Mimi to the art class.

"Claudia and I are giving art lessons," she said. "The kids are making puppets."

"I'm going to make a . . . grrr . . . monster!" said Jamie.

I took over with Mimi and walked her around the table. "We're making papier-mâché," I told her.

"See," said Mimi, nodding wisely.

Since Mimi seemed okay, and the kids who knew her well — Myriah, Gabbie, and Jamie — liked her a lot, I decided it would be okay to let her stay for the class.

"I'll get you a seat, Mimi," I said, eyeing a lawn chair that was folded up in a corner of the basement.

I was struggling to pull the chair out from between the wall and a bicycle, when I heard Mary Anne scream.

I spun around.

Mimi was slithering to the floor at the foot of the stairs. She had fainted again. Luckily she didn't hit her head or anything. The kids looked on in horror, especially Corrie, who kept glancing from Mimi to me. I think she knew somehow that Mimi and I were very close.

And Jamie cried, "Mimi!" and ran to her.

But Mary Anne caught him in her arms and held him in a bear hug for a few seconds to keep him from going near her.

Everything was happening at once. Mary Anne put Corrie, the oldest of the kids, in charge of Jamie. Then she ran to Mimi's side while I dashed upstairs to find my father. As I reached the top step, I could hear Mary Anne say, "Corrie, can you be my helper and take all the kids over to the other side of the room? Ask Jamie to teach you guys his funny song about the big blue frog. Myriah, you help sign to Matt, or he won't understand."

It was amazing. Every kid followed every direction. I know because they were singing and signing, "I'm in love with a big blue frog," when I came back down to the basement with my father.

I had found him in the garage, cleaning up an oil leak from one of our cars. He'd had no idea that Mimi was out of bed, much less dressed and in the basement.

When I found him, I'd cried, "Dad! Dad!" (In my panic, I think I might even have called him "Daddy" like I used to do when I was little.) "Come quick! Right now! Mimi's in the basement and she fainted again."

Dad jumped up in a flash, leaving the oily rag on the floor of the garage. He took the steps down to the basement two at a time, something I'd never seen him do before. When he knelt by Mimi's side (she was still out cold) he began giving orders.

"Claudia, call the paramedics, then find your sister. Mary Anne, take the children home."

He might have sounded cross, but he wasn't. Not really. Just a little panicky.

Mary Anne wisely led the kids out our back basement steps to our side yard. This turned out to be a good decision for two reasons. One, the children didn't have to step over Mimi. Two, they were so fascinated by climbing the flight of dank cement steps, watching Mary Anne push apart the heavy double doors, and emerging into our yard, that they nearly forgot about Mimi.

For the next half hour or so, two things were

going on at once. Mary Anne was dealing with the children, and I was dealing with Mimi. I'll tell you what was going on with Mimi first.

I did just what Dad had told me to do. I ran to the phone in the kitchen and called the paramedics. I was getting pretty good at that. Then I ran through the house, shouting, "Janine! Janine! JANINE!"

"What?" she called. Her voice came from upstairs. She was probably in her room, working on that computer of hers.

"Come downstairs! Mimi's sick again! The ambulance is on its way!"

Sometimes you can't pry Janine away from her computer with a crowbar, but when I told her about Mimi, she came flying out of her room as fast as Dad had left the oil leak in the garage. Then we raced to Mimi.

When Dad saw us coming he said briskly, "You two stay with her, I'll go wait for the ambulance. I think I'll tell the paramedics to use the stairs Mary Anne and the kids used. It'll be easier."

Janine and I stayed with Mimi. I covered her with a blanket that was folded up on the washing machine, and we held her hands and talked to her, just in case she could hear us.

When the paramedics arrived, they lifted

her gently onto the stretcher and carried her up the stairs. I kept waiting for the stretcher to tilt and Mimi to slide off, but somehow the men kept it level.

Meanwhile, Mary Anne and all the children had walked first to Jamie's house and dropped him off, explaining to his parents what had happened. Then they walked back to our neighborhod, where they took Myriah and Gabbie home. Finally, Mary Anne waited outside her house with the remaining kids. It was about time for them to be picked up, and since Mary Anne was just across the street from us, she knew that the parents (or Haley Braddock) would see the children at her house and not come bother us.

However, the children saw the paramedics carry Mimi around from the back of my house and into the ambulance. Mary Anne was glad Jamie and the Perkins girls were at their houses, because they would have been upset. The Arnold twins and Matt were merely curious. But Corrie began to cry.

Mary Anne put her arm around her. "It's going to be okay," she said.

Corrie cried harder. "Claudia must be very sad," she replied.

And Mary Anne thought again that Corrie

seemed to be getting awfully attached to me. She had plenty of time to think about it, too, because it was a good forty-five minutes later, long after the ambulance had left, and Marilyn, Carolyn, and Matt had been picked up, that Mrs. Addison finally arrived.

Mary Anne considered discussing Corrie's and my relationship with me — but not then. Only when things got better. She knew I had plenty to worry about besides Corrie.

# CHAPTER 6

Guess who rode to the hospital in the ambulance with Mimi? I did. Dad decided to take the car, and Janine stayed behind so she could tell our mother what had happened as soon as Mom came home. Janine offered to go with Mimi, but I really wanted to and there was no time for arguing.

I've been in an ambulance before. The last time, I was the patient. I had broken my leg badly. But this time, I was just a passenger. Sometimes the paramedics make the passenger ride up front next to the driver. Sometimes you can beg to sit in back with the patient, which is what I did, and again, no one took the time to argue with me.

I sat on a ledge across from two paramedics, Mimi on the stretcher between us. While the attendants took her blood pressure and stuff,

I just kept holding Mimi's hand and talking to her.

About halfway to the hospital, Mimi woke up and realized what was going on. She was so embarrassed that she tried to make up for it by acting like a grand lady.

"Do I not know father?" she said to one of the attendants. "The honorable Mr. . . . Mr. . . . um . . ."

"I — I don't think so," replied the man. He fiddled with the gauge on the blood pressure instrument.

"But sure. Yes. Live Bradford Court years long ago."

"No, ma'am."

"It's okay, Mimi," I said.

"Oh, my Claudia. You here," said Mimi, turning her head.

"Yes, I'm here." I squeezed her hand a little harder.

"Dinner is not ready," Mimi told me distinctly.

"Don't worry about it," I said. "It's only lunchtime."

"And I never have enough money for payment. Car loan."

I almost pointed out that Mimi hadn't owned a car in years, but decided not to. Besides, we'd reached the hospital.

Here we go again, I thought.


Things were pretty much the same. Mimi got another private room and, by later in the afternoon, our entire family was crowded into it.

Mimi was already better because, remembering her last stay in the hospital, the doctors had given her some new blood.

"Vampire!" exclaimed Mimi, and we laughed, mostly because if Mimi could joke, that was the best sign of all that she was feeling better.

I laughed, too, even though I was madder than I'd ever been. Not at Mimi, not at anyone else in my family, but at the doctors and nurses. Want to know why? I'll tell you why.

This is what happened when Mimi was first taken to her room. She had seemed to be okay in the ambulance and rolling through the hallways of the hospital on the way to her room, but as soon as the attendants transferred her onto her hospital bed which, really, they tried to do as gently as possible, Mimi screamed.

"Oh! Oh!" she cried.

Her entire body stiffened with pain. Dad and I were standing on either side of her bed and we each grabbed one of her hands and held on tight.

"Will someone please get her some pain-killers or something?" my father shouted to whomever was in the room.

Everyone scurried out, but no one came back except a nurse's aide, who took off Mimi's dress and put on a hospital gown instead. She didn't even bother to close the door to the room, so I gave her a dirty look and did it myself.

Mimi's pain seemed to have gone away by then, but Dad asked for the painkillers again anyway.

"I'll see what I can do," the woman replied.

But the next people who came in were Mom and Janine, Mom looking very upset.

"Mother!" she cried, and ran to Mimi. She bent over her. "How are you feeling?"

I think Mimi was about to say, "Fine," when suddenly she went into another one of those awful spasms of pain.

Mom burst into tears.

Dad and I each grabbed one of Mimi's hands again (it was all we could do), and I signaled to Janine to take Mom out of the room. The last thing Mimi needed was to see that she'd upset her daughter. I'm not sure she would have noticed, though. When the pain came, she would arch her back and squinch up her face, closing her eyes.

That darn nurse's aide hadn't put Mimi's hospital gown on very well, I soon realized. Each time Mimi arched her back, the gown slipped further and further down her chest until she was half naked. And Janine had forgotten to close the door behind her when she took Mom out. Anyone in the hall could see right into the room, see Mimi arching her back and squinching her eyes and crying out, with her gown around her waist. I tried to remember her other ways. I imagined her fully dressed, jewelry and all, smiling at me from across the kitchen table as we shared special tea.

After three or four more spasms of pain, Mimi suddenly lay quietly on the bed. I fixed her hospital gown and drew the sheet up to her chin while Dad rang the bell for a nurse for the eighty-eighth time.

"Hey, you guys," I called to Mom and Janine in the hallway. "Come on in. And close the door."

My mother and sister reappeared, Mom with a paper cup full of coffee she'd gotten from a vending machine. She looked an awful lot calmer, even though coffee is supposed to make you hyper or something.

Mom set her coffee cup on Mimi's bedside table and peered over at her mother.

Mimi smiled at her. "All better," she said, and we laughed nervously.

She wasn't, of course. She was so weak she could barely move. When she tried to raise herself to a sitting position, she got dizzy and had to lie down. So we raised the bed for her.

But the pain was gone.

It seemed like hours before anyone bothered to do anything for Mimi, but finally doctors and nurses began showing up. Each time they did, I made sure the door to her room was closed. No more public indignity if I could help it. It was bad enough that our family was standing around while the doctors examined Mimi.

Anyway, they finally gave her those pints of blood, and very soon she announced that she was feeling better. "TV?" she suggested. And not long after that, "Dinner?"

By the next day, Sunday, Mimi was even better — physically. But her mind didn't seem to be working too well. She kept talking about her things at home, about giving them away, as she'd given Mallory the bird. Only she was subtler than that now. On Sunday afternoon, she said, "My Claudia, I would like please to move plants to room. You room."

"Plants?"

"My plants."

"Oh, at home?"

"Yes. Put in room."

"I'll remember to water them," I assured her. "I don't have to move them."

"No. Not that. You have them. Put in room."

"Okay, okay."

Later she told Janine she was afraid someone would steal her diamond earrings while she was away in the hospital. She told her to take them out of her jewelry box and put them in Janine's jewelry box. Or preferably on Janine's ears. That night, I moved the plants and Janine took the earrings.

Mom and Dad asked me to stay with Mimi the following afternoon. So I went to the hospital, even though I had to miss an art class before our club meeting. Mimi was not the funny person she'd been when she'd made the vampire joke on Saturday, nor the anxious person she'd been the day before. On Monday she was confused and cranky. She wandered into the nurses' station and complained that the price of kitty litter was going way up. Then, back in her bed (I practically had to drag her to it), she said crossly, "Turn on TV, Claudia."

I was startled. She hadn't said, "My Claudia."

I turned it on.

"Change. Change channel. No good."

It was a rerun of *Wheel of Fortune*, which is her favorite, but I changed it anyway.

Soon her supper arrived. (It seems like hospital patients get supper around four-thirty.)

"Mess!" said Mimi, scanning her tray. "Trash!" She actually threw a container of bright yellow pudding at the wall. (Well, I might have done the same thing. The pudding looked like a cup of melted yellow crayons.)

Luckily, a doctor came in then to do some more tests on Mimi, since they still didn't know what was wrong with her. I didn't even care that he interrupted her dinner. I was glad for the distraction.

I didn't understand Mimi at all. Especially not when, after the doctor left, Mimi seemed to be her sweet self again and told me, "My Claudia, never believe what other people say. About you. Never unless you believe it, too. I love you."

"I love you, too, Mimi," I said, forgetting entirely that just a while ago I'd wanted to take her by her shoulders and shake her for being such a baby and throwing her pudding at the wall.

That night, Corrie called me twice. She didn't really have much to say. I think she just wanted to talk. And I wanted somebody who needed my sympathy, since Mimi didn't seem to want much of mine. When I'd left the hospital that afternoon, I'd said, "Feel better soon," and she hadn't even answered. I don't know why.

But guess what happened on Tuesday — the doctors said Mimi could go home the next day! They couldn't figure out what was wrong and didn't see any reason to keep her in the hospital. I was so excited, I called all my friends with the news. I even called Corrie, who said, "Oh, Claudia! That's great! You must be so happy. I can't wait to see you on Saturday!"

Mom and Dad and Janine and I ate a celebratory dinner that night. Later, as Janine and I were cleaning up the kitchen, Janine suddenly turned to me and gave me a hug. We hardly ever hug.

"What's up?" I asked her, smiling.

"I'm relieved about Mimi. Aren't you?"

"Definitely!"

I went to my room to work on my stop-action painting, and a few minutes later, my phone rang.

It was Mimi!

She sounded fine and we chatted for a long time. I told Mimi how the painting was coming along.

At last she said, "Well, let you go now. Do not want to confuse the Muses."

I had no idea what she meant, so I just said, "See you tomorrow, Mimi."

"Good-bye, my Claudia."

# CHAPTER 7

On school days, our family gets up at six-thirty. So I was surprised, on Wednesday morning, to hear voices and people moving around, and to look at my digital clock and see that it read 4:52.

Four fifty-two? What was going on?

I had to go to the bathroom anyway, so I got up. But I never even reached the bathroom. The noise and commotion was coming from my parents' bedroom. I stopped at their door. I know it isn't nice, but I listened to their voices for a few moments. All I could catch were snatches of conversation.

I heard Dad say, ". . . arrangements to make."

Then I heard Mom say (and did she sound as if she were crying?) "I can't believe it." (A pause.) ". . . have to tell the girls."

I drew in a deep breath, knowing something

was very wrong, and knocked on their door.

My father opened it. He was dressed except for his socks, which he was struggling to put on, hopping around on one foot, and at the same time, reaching for his wallet and stuffing it in his pocket.

Behind him, my mother was hurriedly pulling a blouse on over her slip. A pair of stockings and her pocketbook had been tossed on the bed, which was unmade.

Maybe I've made a mistake, I thought. Maybe the clock actually said 9:52 and we were all late for work and school. But no. Mom and Dad's clock now said 4:54.

"Mom? Dad?" I said. "What's going on?"

I realized then that my mother *was* crying. She sank into a chair and opened her arms to me, inviting me to sit in her lap, which I hadn't done in years. But I did it then anyway.

Mom took my hand and said, "Claudia, Mimi died during the night. Just a little while ago."

I think my heart stopped beating then. I really do. I think it missed two beats. When it began working properly again, I felt my stomach turn to ice.

"I don't believe it," I whispered. "She was fine last night."

I felt my father's hand on the back of my head. He stroked my hair. "No, she wasn't," he said, and choked on the words. "She wasn't fine, honey. Not really. She was old and she was sick. I think she just wore out."

All I could do was nod my head.

After that, the morning was pandemonium. The early morning, that is. I had to get out of Mom's lap because she and Dad had to finish dressing and rush to the hospital to do whatever you do there when someone you love dies. But first they had to wake up Janine and tell her, so there were more tears and hugs.

When Mom and Dad finally drove off, Janine and I sat at the kitchen table with cups of tea. We did not use Mimi's special cups. In fact, before our tea, I closed the door to Mimi's room so we wouldn't have to look at her things.

Janine and I had been told that we could stay home from school, so we just sat at the table. After a very long silence, I said, "I talked to Mimi on the phone last night. You know what her last words to me were? I mean, before she said, 'Good-bye, my Claudia'?"

Janine shook her head. "What were they?"

"She said she'd let me go now. She didn't want to confuse the Muses."

Janine smiled. "Were you working on a painting or something?"

I nodded. "The stop-action painting. I was telling Mimi about it."

"Mimi meant to say that she didn't want to *disturb* the Muses."

"I don't get it. What are the Muses?"

"The Muses are, well, they're creative forces. They're spirits or powers that are supposed to inspire artists and musicians and writers. Disturbing the Muses means interrupting a creative person at work. Mimi just got the phrase mixed up."

"Oh." I knew Janine would have an explanation. She always does. But I was really thinking about Mimi. She was the only one in my family who had understood about my art and how *very* important it is to me, and how serious I am about it.

And now she was gone.

Suddenly, I felt alone and abandoned, like Corrie waiting on our front steps for her mother. It's funny to feel abandoned with your own sister sitting across the table from you.

Janine looked at her watch. I looked at mine. Mom and Dad had told us that at seven o'clock we should begin phoning relatives and close friends to tell them what had happened. The funeral would be on Saturday, in just three days, and there was a lot to do before then.

So at seven, Janine took over the phone in the kitchen to call our relatives, and I went upstairs to my own phone to call my friends. I knew that if I called just the families of the Baby-sitters Club members, word would travel fast (it always does in a small town), and soon anyone else who should hear the news, like the Newtons, would hear it.

I sat on my bed with my back to the windowsill so I wouldn't have to look at Mimi's plants.

I called Mary Anne first. That was going to be the hardest of the calls because Mary Anne had been almost as close to Mimi as I'd been. Growing up without a mother, she had come to Mimi with skinned knees or for advice or to learn a new knitting stitch.

"Mary Anne?" I said when she picked up the phone, sounding not quite awake. It was 7:03.

"Claud?" she replied. "Is anything wrong?" (Mary Anne has emotional antennae.)

"Mimi died last night." I had to say it that way. I couldn't hedge with Mary Anne. "She died in the hospital. Mom and Dad are over there now," (my voice broke), "getting her things and — and — "

Mary Anne was already crying, so I didn't see any reason to keep talking.

"I'm sorry, Claud," she said, between sobs.

I began to cry again, too. "So am I. I know how close you were."

When Mary Anne calmed down a little, she offered to call the other members of the club for me, which was very nice of her. I let her call Dawn (so Dawn could console Mary Anne) and Jessi and Mal. But I wanted to call Kristy and Stacey myself.

I called Stacey first. Stacey hadn't been close to Mimi at all, but she'd known her and liked her, and besides, Stacey was my best friend. I *had* to call her.

Stacey was getting ready to leave for school when the phone rang in her New York apartment. She was supposed to be out the door twenty minutes from when I was calling. But she stopped and talked anyway. She knew, as soon as she heard my voice at that hour on a weekday, that something was wrong.

"Mimi died early this morning," I told her flatly. Each time I said that, the words came a little more easily — but they didn't seem any more real. I was calling people, telling them Mimi was dead, and not believing it myself.

Maybe that was because I suddenly realized that I didn't know what "dead" meant. Oh, sure, I understood that it meant not breathing or thinking or moving or feeling; the opposite of alive. But what did it *really* mean?

Stacey was comforting at first, and then began asking questions. "When is the funeral? What time? Which church?" She and her parents were going to come, of course, she said, before we got off the phone.

The call to Kristy was easier than the others had been. Kristy is not a crier. She'd known Mimi for as long as Mary Anne and I had, since the three of us had grown up together (at least before Kristy moved), and she loved Mimi, but she wasn't as close to her as Mary Anne and I had been. I guess she hadn't needed her quite as much as we had. Besides, she has Nannie, her own wonderful grandmother.

Still, Kristy was shocked, and after all the "I'm sorry's" and "What can I do's?" she said, "Our club meeting this afternoon is canceled, of course. I'll tell the rest of the members in school today."

"Oh, no! Please," I said hurriedly. "Don't

cancel it. I want to see you guys tonight. Don't stay away from me. I need you. I mean," I babbled on, "even if we don't conduct an official meeting, please let's just all be together. Mom and Dad won't mind. I don't think. We'll stay up in my room."

"Wow, okay," said Kristy, sounding breathless, even though I had just done all the talking. "I didn't mean for you to think we'd, you know, shut you out. We wouldn't do that. I just figured today would be sort of a private one for your family. But if you want us there, we'll be there."

I felt a little better by the time we hung up.

But not much. Before I left my bedroom I took this framed portrait of Mimi that I had once painted down from the wall and slid it under my bed. Then I decided I didn't want Mimi under my bed, so I put her in my closet. But I didn't want her in my closet, either, so I moved her to the attic and left her there.

Kristy had said she thought that day would be a private one for us. She couldn't have been more wrong. Word about Mimi's death spread fast (as I'd thought it would), and people began coming over to our house around eleven o'clock. And everyone who dropped by

69

brought food. Why? Because Mimi had been the cook in our family? That didn't make sense. The rest of us could cook, too. Anyway, our relatives came (with food) and helped Mom and Dad make funeral arrangements and write Mimi's obituary. Our neighbors and friends dropped by to console us.

It was the longest day of my life. If I hadn't believed it before, I became more and more certain, each time the doorbell rang, that Mimi really and truly had died. (Whatever that meant.)

I wished everyone would go away and leave us alone and let me think that a big mistake had been made.

But at five-thirty, my parents left to meet with our minister, all the visitors left, too, and my friends came over. We held a strange meeting. For one thing, Janine sat in on it because she didn't want to be alone. For another thing, it wasn't really a meeting. Kristy didn't conduct business. She didn't wear her visor. She didn't even sit in the director's chair. And no one called because all our clients knew what had happened and figured we wouldn't be holding a meeting. They didn't want to intrude, anyway. So the seven of us sat on the floor. We barely spoke because no one seemed to know what to say after, "I'm sorry," and, "We'll really miss her."

But we were together.

Even so, the longer we sat there, the guiltier I felt. I couldn't help remembering the times I'd lost my temper, wished to be at an art class instead of at the hospital — and especially the time I'd thrown the magazines on Mimi's bed.

I was a horrible person and I knew it, even if no one else did.

# CHAPTER 8

Friday

I was surprised that we held our regular club meeting today, but I was glad, too. I was glad because it gave me a chance to see that you really seem okay, Claudia. In fact, you act almost like nothing happened. And that seems fine to me. I'm happy to see you get back to normal so quickly. I was also surprised to hear that you and Mary Ann will be holding your Saturday art class on Sunday, the day after Mimi's funeral, but, hey -- great. Maybe the best thing to do is just jump right back into your routine.

The reason this notebook entry is not about a baby-sitting job is because there hasn't been much to write about the last couple of days.

No one has called us. I think they're being polite and waiting until after the funeral.

Claud, I'm glad you're feeling so much better. If you hadn't been, Friday night might never have happened, and it was such a great night that I wouldn't have missed it for the world....

Despite what Kristy wrote in the notebook, I know she felt a little funny holding a club meeting on Friday, the day before Mimi's funeral, but I really wanted to. Janine and I weren't going back to school until Monday because there was too much to do at home. And with everything all out of order like that, I at *least* wanted to hold regular club meetings, and Mom and Dad had given their permission. I didn't like special attention. I wanted my life to go on as usual, or, as Kristy said, as if nothing had happened. That was pretty difficult when I wasn't going to school, so if we'd stopped our club meetings, I don't know what I'd have done.

Kristy was right. Our Friday meeting was quiet, like the one on Wednesday. No one called. Plus, us club members didn't seem to know what to talk about at first. Finally, Kristy started talking about food fights and bras, trying to make us laugh (Janine was *not* at that meeting), and that worked for awhile.

At ten minutes of six, Mary Anne stood up. "Come on," she said. "I'm starved. There's no point in sitting around here. Let's go to my house now and order the pizzas."

Mary Anne had invited the club members to her house for a pizza dinner, since her dad and Dawn's mom were going out on a *date*, and she had already invited Dawn over to keep her company. Besides, Mary Anne thought I might *need* a pizza supper with my friends on the night before Mimi's funeral. (I think Mary Anne needed it, too. She'd been pretty teary lately. In fact, she seemed even more upset than I did. I hadn't cried since Wednesday morning.)

So the six of us left my house and walked across the street to Mary Anne's dark, empty one. She turned on the porch light, unlocked the front door, turned on the inside hall light, and was greeted by Tigger, her kitten.

Kristy told me later that she thought it must be really lonely sometimes to be Mary Anne. Was it possible, I wondered, that Mary Anne would miss Mimi even more than I would?

"Hiya, Tiggy. Hi there, Mousekin." (Mousekin is also Tigger. Mary Anne has about a zillion nicknames for him.) She picked Tigger up and nuzzled him under her chin. "I bet you're hungry, aren't you? Well, so are we. Kristy, why don't you order the pizzas while I feed Tigger?"

We had to have a very long conversation about what kinds of pizzas to get since we can all be picky about some foods. Dawn wouldn't eat anything but plain or with vegetables like green peppers. No one else likes green peppers. I wanted a pizza with everything, but Jessi gagged at the thought of anchovies. Mary Anne didn't want sausage. We did finally order two pizzas, though, and when they arrived, they were actually hot. (Pizza Express isn't always as express as they advertise.)

We crowded around the Spiers' kitchen table with the open boxes of pizzas in the middle and started grabbing slices, the cheese stringing out from each slice, still attached to the pies. We didn't bother with plates. A pile of napkins was good enough for us.

In the middle of a big bite of pizza, Kristy began to laugh.

"What?" said the rest of us.

Kristy managed to swallow before she answered. "Remember the time Mimi tasted her first pizza?"

No one seemed aghast that Kristy had brought up the subject of Mimi. In fact, it seemed sort of appropriate, especially since this was a particularly good story.

"*I* do!" I cried. "That was so funny."

"Let's tell Mimi stories!" exclaimed Kristy.

"Okay," my friends and I agreed.

"What about the pizza?" asked Mallory.

I looked at Kristy. "You tell," I said. "You were there."

"Okay," she replied. "Well, it was Claudia's eighth birthday, and Mimi's present to her was going to be a meal at a real Japanese restaurant in Stamford. She wanted to take Claudia, her family, and Mary Anne and me. Mary Anne and I were *so excited*. We'd never had Japanese food before. We'd barely even been in a fancy restaurant. So we got all dressed up in, like, birthday party clothes — so did you, Claud — and everyone *else* was dressed up, and *Mimi* was wearing an actual Japanese outfit — "

"Authentic," I said importantly.

"You know, the kimono and the sandals and everything."

"We were fascinated," Mary Anne added.

"So," Kristy continued, "we drive all the way to Stamford and the restaurant is *closed*. No one can believe it. So we begin driving around looking for other places to eat."

"Oh, and remember," said Mary Anne, "we passed a Howard Johnson's and Mr. Kishi said we could go in there to eat because he knew the manager personally, and I thought he meant he knew *Howard Johnson*. I was so impressed."

Everyone giggled at that.

"Well," said Kristy, "we couldn't find a place where Claud and Mary Anne and I wanted to eat. I mean, they were all, like, French places with these frou-frou names, and it *was* Claud's birthday, so when she finally said she wanted pizza, Mr. Kishi stopped at the first pizza place he saw. It was kind of sleazy — dark, with a lot of high school kids being loud — and a miniature juke box playing at every booth. But we went in anyway."

"And everyone stared," I said, "because Mimi looked like she was on her way to a costume party, but we ordered two pies anyway, and Mimi ate one slice very bravely."

"*And*," said Kristy, "as we were finally leaving that awful place where everyone had been staring at us, Mimi turned around, faced the people in the restaurant, and announced, "Best Japanese food I have ever eaten!"

Us club members were hysterical. Jessi even dropped a whole slice of pizza on the floor.

"Tell everyone about Russ and Peaches," Mary Anne suddenly said to me.

"Russ and Peaches?" repeated Dawn.

"My aunt and uncle," I replied.

"Mimi had a son and she named him *Russ*?" said Dawn incredulously. "That just sounds so . . . unconventional. I mean, for Mimi. . . . Russ."

"Well, his real name is Russell," I told her, "but he isn't Mimi's son. And he's American. I mean, *American* American."

"So you're saying Mimi named your mother's sister *Peaches*?" squeaked Mallory. "That's even wor — even more unconventional."

"Oh, no," I said quickly. "My aunt has a Japanese name, but Russ started calling her Peaches and she just called him Russ, so everyone else calls them Russ and Peaches, too. Janine and I never even call them 'Aunt' and 'Uncle.' "

"I remember them," said Kristy.

"Yeah, they used to live in Stoneybrook, right?" added Mary Anne.

I nodded. "Until I was about seven. You'll see them at the, um — the funeral tomorrow."

"They were really wild," said Kristy. "It's hard to believe Peaches is Mimi's daughter."

"It's even harder to believe she married Russ," I said. "Remember the time we had that *huge* storm?" I said to Kristy and Mary Anne. "It was practically a hurricane. It closed school, and Stoneybrook didn't have any electricity for two days, and all the phone lines were down."

"Yeah. We were in, what? First grade?" asked Kristy.

"I think so," I replied. "Anyway, Russ wanted to make sure Mimi and our family were okay, only he couldn't drive to our house because trees were down everywhere, and he couldn't walk because he'd broken his ankle in a shelving accident. (Don't ask.) So he rode over in a *golf cart!*"

Everyone burst out laughing.

"I remember another time," I said, "when Mimi could still drive, and she was on her way to the grocery store and an ambulance pulled out in front of her, and suddenly Mimi decided she was going to be an ambulance chaser. So she puts on the speed and follows the ambulance, and where do you think it goes?"

"Where?" asked my friends.

"To Russ and Peaches' house! Peaches had fallen down the stairs. Mimi never chased another ambulance."

More giggling.

"I also remember when we realized that Mimi couldn't be allowed to drive anymore," I went on. "It wasn't so long ago. She was pulling up to an intersection and she slowed down, peered at the stoplight, glanced at Mom, and said, 'Honey, tell me. That light — is it red or is it green?' "

"Tell about the chicken dinner!" Mallory suddenly cried. "I like *that* story."

"Oh, yeah," I said slowly, remembering. "We were having a dinner party — Mal's parents were there — and all the guests were seated in the dining room and Dad very proudly carries in this platter with a beautiful roast chicken on it. But he trips and the chicken slides off the platter and falls on the floor. Mom is turning beet-red, but you know what Mimi does? She just says very calmly, 'That is all right. Bring in other chicken, son.' Well, of course there was no other chicken, but Dad got the message. He scooped the spilled chicken back onto the platter, took it into the kitchen, fixed it up, and returned it to the dining room."

"Mimi saved the day!" said Jessi, grinning.

The phone rang then and Mary Anne answered. She listened for a moment, said, "Okay, just a sec," then cupped her hand over the receiver and whispered, "Claud, it's for you. It's Corrie. She called your house first and found out you were here."

I nodded. When I took the phone from Mary Anne, I said cheerfully to Corrie, "Hi, kid. How are you doing?"

"Fine," said Corrie, not sounding fine at all. "I miss you."

"I miss you, too. But I'll see you on Sunday. Remember? We'll be having our art class on Sunday this weekend instead of Saturday."

"I remember."

"What are you doing?"

"Staying away from our baby-sitter. Mommy and Daddy are at a party. They got this old lady to come over because they didn't want to bother you. I don't like the lady. Neither does Sean. She smells funny."

"Tell her you're tired and that you're going

to bed," I suggested. "Then you can just play in your room. That's what I used to do when I didn't like my baby-sitters."

"Oh, good idea!"

Corrie and I got off the phone, and soon us sitters had to go home. Kristy told me several days later that, as we were leaving, she could feel our spirits sinking. We'd had fun telling Mimi stories. We'd remembered her the way she would have wanted to be remembered. But the next day would be the funeral, and it would not be happy or funny.

How, Kristy wondered, how on *earth* would we get through Mimi's funeral?

I was wondering the same thing.

# CHAPTER 9

Saturday

I am writing in my New York branch of the Baby-Sitters Club notebook. (I keep a notebook even though I'm the only one in the club.) I didn't do any sitting today, that's for sure, but I felt that the day should be recorded somehow, and my baby-sitting notebook seemed like a good place to record in, since if it hadn't been for sitting, I probably wouldn't have gotten to know Mimi as well as I did.

Today was Mimi's funeral. It was a very sad, difficult day. I'm sure there are some better, bigger words to describe how Claudia was feeling, but I can't think of any. Just sad, bad, low, etc.

Anyway, the day started when Mom and I left for Stoneybrook this morning.

Stacey and her mother decided to drive to Stoneybrook instead of taking the train. That way, they wouldn't need anyone to pick them up at the train station, and they could go back whenever they wanted. Also, Mr. McGill likes to drive. Only he decided, at the very last minute, not to come to the funeral. I was a little hurt when I saw just Stacey and her mom get out of the car, but then I thought, Well, Mr. McGill hadn't known Mimi very well. It wasn't until later that Stacey told me, pretty reluctantly, that she'd heard her parents arguing the night before. She thought maybe they needed a day apart from each other. Besides, her mother has always liked Stoneybrook better than her father did. He's happier in the city.

Stacey said the ride to Connecticut was pretty quiet. She had a feeling her mother was thinking about her father. And Stacey was thinking about me. Plus, they were both sad about Mimi, of course.

The McGills arrived at the cemetery right on time. Mimi's burial was to be held before the funeral service, so the McGills just joined the long line of cars that were driving slowly through the cemetery and parking by the side of the road. I watched Stacey and her mother climb out and stretch their legs.

All I wanted to do then was run to Stacey and hug her, but a funny thing had happened that morning.

Our family had woken up formal.

We began the day formally, Janine and I following all sorts of somber instructions from our parents, and we spent the rest of the morning being formal.

When Stacey arrived, her first sight was of the plot where Mimi was to be buried. The casket was sitting next to the open grave, and Mom and Dad, Janine and I, Russ and Peaches, and a few other family members were standing nearest to the casket. Friends and neighbors were behind us. I turned my head and saw Stacey, and we looked at each other.

But I could not run to her, and she could not come to me.

She and her mother joined Kristy, her mother, and her older brothers Sam and Charlie, at the back of the crowd.

The burial service began. It was quite short, but Stacey remembers much more about it than I do. All I remember is thinking, as the casket was being lowered into the ground, Mimi's not in there. So I didn't cry. A bunch of men were just putting a box in the ground. That was all. Then Mom made me throw a white rose into the hole. I thought, What's the point? Mimi won't see it. But I did it anyway (since we were being formal).

Stacey remembers more. She remembers the minister saying some words about Mimi and then saying a blessing over the casket. And she remembers that the graveyard was silent, except for the minister, because no one was ready to cry yet. A burial is just too separate from the memory of the dead person.

It is surreal.

Stacey remembers the rest of the service and then everyone slowly walking back to their cars and driving to the church for the funeral.

I don't remember any of that. It is a blank for me. I dropped the silly flower in the hole — and then suddenly I was in the church, in the front pew with my family.

The thing I learned about death that day is that if it's *your* relative, *you* always get to be in front. Maybe that's to help you feel closer to the dead person.

Stacey also remembers the funeral service better than I do. My mom gave the eulogy, and she referred to Mimi as either "Mother" or "Mimi" throughout the whole talk, which was nice because almost everybody knew her simply as Mimi. Everyone who was at the funeral, I mean, and according to Stacey an awful lot of people were there: all the members of the Baby-sitters Club, even Logan (but not Shannon; she didn't know Mimi), and most of their parents. Then there were people like the Newtons and the Perkinses and our next-door neighbors, the Goldmans, and of course all the rest of our relatives. (You could tell how closely related they were to Mimi by how near the front of the church they got to sit.)

Stacey said that not many kids came to the funeral, and I think that's okay. Little children probably wouldn't understand what was going on, and there's plenty of time for them to learn about death when they're older.

Later I wondered who had baby-sat for all those kids. Probably smelly old ladies. I guess we're not the only baby-sitters in Stoneybrook.

Stacey and her mom sat in a pew sort of in the middle of the church. Also in their pew were Mary Anne and her father, Dawn and her mother, Kristy and her mother, and Sam and Charlie. (Watson didn't come because he had barely known Mimi, so he stayed at home and helped Kristy's grandmother watch the little kids.) In the pew in front of Stacey were

Mallory and her parents and Jessi and her parents. Stacey said that, much as she thought the girls in the club needed comfort then, they suddenly found that they could hardly even look at each other. Stacey was seated right next to Mary Anne, who started to cry buckets as soon as my mother began the eulogy, but she didn't reach for Mary Anne's hand and Mary Anne didn't reach for hers — or for her father's. She just cried silently and kept pulling dry tissues out of her purse and dropping wet ones back into it.

Stacey didn't cry. She said she felt like a stone.

That was a very good description. It was exactly how I felt.

And *that* made me feel guilty on top of everything else. All around me, my relatives were crying. Next to me, Janine, who was wearing Mimi's diamond earrings, was sniffling. On the other side of me, my dad even started to cry and then I almost panicked. I'd never seen him cry before. (What do you do when your father cries?) Even my mother cried a little while she was speaking.

I felt like I just didn't have any tears in me, but that I owed it to Mimi to cry, so I thought about how I had thrown the magazines on her bed, which did bring a few tears of shame to my eyes. I dabbed at them with a Kleenex and hoped that if Mimi could see me from somewhere, she would notice me crying, but not know *why* I was crying. Then I began to wonder if she'd want me to be sad in the first place. It was too confusing.

I didn't pay a bit of attention to any of the service. When it was over, I just stood up and filed into an anteroom, following in Janine's formal footsteps.

In the anteroom, our family formed a line and greeted the other mourners. At last Stacey and I could be together — for a few seconds. We hugged, and Stacey said, "See you at your house later."

There was going to be a reception at our house in about an hour, in just enough time for Mom and Dad, Russ and Peaches, Janine and me to finish greeting people, rush home, and set out all the food everyone had been bringing by since Wednesday. I couldn't wait. I was hoping the formality would wear off during the reception and I could be with my friends.

The formality did wear off. Mom and Dad

let us club members go in the den with a platter of food and talk by ourselves. Logan came, too.

But talk? At first no one knew what to say. Stacey told me weeks and weeks later that it was because everything had already been said. At first it had been, "I'm sorry," and, "Oh, how terrible," and, "Poor Claudia. You must feel so awful." Then we had told our Mimi stories. What else was left to say on the subject? Was it okay *not* to talk about Mimi? Was it okay to tell Stacey about school or for Mary Anne to talk about Tigger?

Tentatively, we tried it on, like a dress we weren't sure we wanted to buy. It seemed to fit okay. So we sat in the den with our food, and Mallory said that the weekend before, one of the triplets had secretly stuck a target on the back of Claire's T-shirt and gleefully spent Saturday shooting things at her. We laughed.

Then I said, "Hey, Stace, Dorrie Wallingford is going out with a freshman in *high school!*"

"No!" cried Stacey, with a gasp.

"Well, I'm leaving," said Logan, who always leaves when we start talking about boy-girl things.

Slowly the other club members left, too. They couldn't stay all afternoon. But Stacey was the last to leave. Her mom very nicely let the two of us have a long visit.

"I put Mimi's portrait in the attic," I confessed to Stacey.

"That's okay," she assured me. "Maybe you'll take it out again someday."

"It was like she was watching me or something."

Stacey nodded, but I don't know if she really understood what I meant.

I didn't dwell on that, though. Mrs. McGill came into the den then and said that they really did have to start home.

So Stacey and I hugged and hugged, but when she left, we found that we could not say good-bye.

# CHAPTER 10

$B$ack to school.

Usually I hate going back to school after a weekend or a vacation or even after I've been out sick for a few days. But this time I practically couldn't wait to get there. I was tired of people dropping by our house and not knowing what to say about Mimi. I was tired of flowers and sympathy cards. And I thought that if I saw one more pound cake I would barf. I, the junk food addict, had had enough cake and cookies for the first time ever.

All I wanted was something normal — a day like last Tuesday when Mimi was still alive, which was less than a week ago. I wanted to walk to Stoneybrook Middle School with Mary Anne, open the side door, which we sometimes use because it's close to my locker, saunter through the halls, look for the other club members or maybe for Dorrie Wallingford or

Ashley Wyeth or some other friend, and hope that a boy would notice my outfit and smile at me.

That was not exactly what happened.

Mary Anne and I reached school and we separated because she needed to go talk to her English teacher. So I walked to my locker alone. Then, since the first bell wasn't going to ring for about ten more minutes, I sort of toured the halls. I was itching for friends, gossip, boys, anything normal. But something weird was going on.

No one would talk to me. No one would even look at me.

I saw Dorrie down a hall on the second floor and waved to her. She turned and walked in the other direction, pretending she hadn't seen me. I *know* she was pretending. It was obvious.

Then I practically bumped into Ashley Wyeth.

"Hi!" I cried.

Now, I know Ashley's mind is usually on another planet, but I can always bring her back to earth for a conversation.

Not this time.

All she did was sort of mumble, "Oh, hi," and walk away.

She didn't say, "It's good to have you back," or, "I'm sorry about your grandmother," or even just, "I missed you."

I didn't want a lot of sympathy about Mimi. Frankly, I wanted to forget the past five days and the fact that she was dead. But Ashley could have said *some*thing . . . couldn't she? Even, "Here's all the homework you missed," would have been better than, "Oh, hi," and walking away.

But Ashley wasn't the only one who did things like that. It went on all morning with the kids I hadn't seen since Tuesday.

I couldn't wait for lunch, which the older members of the BSC always eat together. If nothing else, they would talk to me.

"What is going *on?*" I exploded as soon as we were settled at our usual table. I told them about Dorrie and Ashley and the morning. "In the halls, people look away from me," I added. "They look at the floor, the walls, their books, everywhere but at me. It's like I'm a leper. Wait a sec. . . . Did my nose fall off or something?" I put my hand up to my face and felt around for it. "Nope. Couldn't be that. My nose is still there."

We giggled. Then Dawn said, "Maybe the kids just don't know what to say. They *do* know how close you and Mimi were. It's almost as if one of your parents had died. Maybe they think *anything* they say won't be enough. Or that it will sound stupid."

"Maybe they think you'll get too much attention," spoke up Kristy. "You know, your teachers will say, 'Take your time making up your work,' and stuff like that."

But it was Mary Anne who said quietly, "Maybe they're afraid something like this will happen to *them* now. They see that people you love *do* die."

We grew silent, thinking about that. Finally, Logan broke the ice by saying, "Well, Claudia's not catching!"

I might as well have been, though. The rest of the week wasn't much better than Monday had been, although by Friday, some kids would at least *look* at me. Maybe in a way, this new problem was good. I know that sounds funny, but it was something to help keep my mind off Mimi. And I was looking for any distraction I could find. I concentrated on my art — my stop-action painting — and baby-sitting and even my schoolwork. Often, I did my homework without being told. I don't think I did it very well, but at least I did it — usually. When I couldn't concentrate, I painted or called Stacey or thought about Corrie or about how weird the kids at school were being.

Sometimes I forgot that Mimi was dead. Like, one morning, I woke up to the smell of coffee and thought, Mimi's already in the kitchen. And one afternoon I was in a card store and suddenly thought, almost in a panic, Mimi's birthday is only a week away and I don't have a card or a present for her. Each time, the awful truth would then blaze its way back into my brain.

Other times, I wouldn't be thinking about Mimi at all, and her memory would come crashing back to me. Those times were the most inconvenient, because I wanted to forget, not remember. Once, I was listening to the radio, and a song was playing and there was a line in it about a gentle person or a gentle life or something like that, and it brought Mimi to mind right away.

I only let myself cry for a couple of minutes, though.

Boy, was I glad when Saturday rolled around. I'm always glad to see the weekend, but now Saturday also meant the art class and Corrie and all the other kids. Mary Anne and Corrie usually arrived early and around the same time, so I would let Corrie help Mary Anne and me set things up for the lesson. We were still working on the papier-mâché puppets.

That morning, Corrie arrived before Mary Anne did.

"Hi, Claudia," she greeted me at the door. I always get the feeling that Corrie is more excited than she sounds. Like she's holding back, afraid to let people see how she's really feeling. I wondered what Corrie thought would happen if she let go a little bit.

"Hiya!" I said, giving her a quick hug.

"How are you feeling?" asked Corrie. She had been very concerned ever since Mimi died.

"I'm fine. I really am," I replied, even though I wasn't. But I didn't feel like talking about Mimi. I just wanted to work on the puppets.

Corrie looked relieved.

Mary Anne showed up then, so the three of us set out the partly finished puppets, the paint, the papier-mâché, and the odds and ends and scraps. The kids were at all stages with their puppets, some still applying layers of papier-mâché, other beginning to paint on faces.

The rest of the kids trickled in and soon we were hard at work.

"You know what it's time for you to do today?" I said to Jamie.

"What?"

"Pop your balloon." (Once the papier-mâché is dry, you stick a pin in the bottom of the balloon, then pull the balloon out through what will be the neck of the puppet.)

"Oh! Oh, goody!" For some reason, popping the balloons seemed to be everybody's favorite part of the project.

Marilyn had been the first and she had actually squealed with happiness.

Mary Anne had grinned at me after that class. "You'd have thought Marilyn had died and gone to . . ." She'd trailed off, blushing. "Sorry," she'd mumbled.

Now Jamie popped his balloon with great glee.

"Okay, you're ready to paint your puppet's head," I told him. "But be careful. Remember that papier-mâché is fragile. Your puppet's head is hollow."

Jamie nodded solemnly.

"What color are you going to paint him?" asked Gabbie, who had painted the face of her

Cabbage Patch doll a pale shade of blue.

"Green, what else?" replied Jamie.

"How are you doing, Corrie?" I asked, as Mary Anne and I walked slowly around the table, checking on things.

"Fine, thank you," she replied politely. She held up Nancy Drew. "See?" She was working slowly and carefully. She'd even brought along two Nancy Drew books so she could use pictures of her heroine as models.

I don't like making comparisons between kids, and any comparison between Corrie and this group would have been unfair since Corrie was the oldest student, but I have to say that Corrie's puppet was far and away the best one in the class. It was better than most nine-year-olds would have made.

"It's better than I could do," Mary Anne whispered to me.

When class was over, the materials put away, the puppets propped up to dry, and the children — except for Corrie — gone, she and I sat out on our front steps and waited for her mother. We weren't talking, and I caught Corrie smiling a private smile.

I tickled her and she giggled.

"What was making you smile?" I asked her.

"My puppet," she replied. "I love it. I am going to give it to my mother. Not for any special occasion. Just to please her. I know it will please her."

And Corrie smiled happily again.

# CHAPTER 11

Kristy's visor was on. Her pencil was over her ear. She was sitting ramrod straight in my director's chair.

You guessed it. Time for another club meeting.

"Order, please," said Kristy, and the rest of us settled down.

It was a Wednesday, so there were no dues to collect.

"Any club business?" asked Kristy.

"I move that I find my bag of Cheetos," I said, and everyone giggled.

I was pretty sure it was under my bed, so I lay down on the floor and began searching around among shoe boxes and things. I remembered hiding Mimi's portrait under there temporarily, but put the thought out of my head right away. I was getting pretty good at that lately, even though I seemed to feel more tired than I'd ever felt in my life.

Maybe I was coming down with the flu. Or leprosy.

"Here they are!" I said, emerging triumphantly with the bag.

"That's club business?" asked Kristy.

"It is when we're all starving," I told her.

Luckily for me, the phone rang then.

We lined up one job, the phone rang a second time, and we lined up another job.

The meeting hit a lull, so I asked Kristy, "How's Emily?"

Kristy looked rapturous, like a woman with her newborn baby. "Oh, she's *wonderful!*" she exclaimed. "She's learning to speak so *fast*. Of course, we're all teaching her, so she's got nine teachers. Even Andrew goes around the house with her, pointing to things, and saying, '*Book*, Emily. Say *book*.' or 'Pen. This is a *pen*, Emily.' I'm not sure how much Vietnamese she could speak, but she's sure learning English fast. Guess what her favorite word is?"

"What?" asked Mallory.

"Cookie," replied Kristy. "And she usually gets one when she says it."

"I hope you're not going to spoil her," said Dawn.

"We're trying not to. Anyway, I don't think

Nannie will let us. I am *so* glad she moved in instead of some housekeeper. At first, I thought a housekeeper would be good. I thought she would make my bed for me and stuff, but we all decided it would be a little weird having a stranger live in our house. Besides, Nannie was tired of living alone, and I don't blame her. She's too vivacious. She needs people around her. So the arrangement works out perfectly. We cleared out the room we would have given the housekeeper, gave it to Nannie instead, she moved her things in, and now Nannie takes care of Emily while Mom and Watson are at work, and the rest of us are at school. After school, us kids are on our own as usual, because Nannie has a million and one things to do: bowling practice, visiting friends, you know."

"It's so funny to see the Pink Clinker parked in Watson's driveway," spoke up Mary Anne.

"I know." (The Pink Clinker is Kristy's grandmother's old car. She really did have it painted pink, and it really does clink around a lot when she drives it, but it seems to be in good shape.)

Kristy knows her grandmother as well as I knew Mimi, although I'm not sure they're as close. Nannie's husband has been dead for

103

quite awhile, and Kristy hardly ever sees her father's parents. (I don't know what she thinks of Watson's parents.)

"Hey," said Mallory suddenly, "Mary Anne, what's going on with your father and Dawn's mother?"

I thought Mal was being a little nosy (even though I was dying to know myself), but Mary Anne and Dawn just looked at each other and grinned.

"Mom is not seeing the Trip-Man as often," Dawn replied gleefully. (Mrs. Schafer has been dating this man nicknamed Trip, whom Dawn can't stand and calls the Trip-Man.)

"And Dad doesn't see anyone but Mrs. Schafer," said Mary Anne with a grin.

"I don't get it, though," said Dawn, frowning suddenly. "Our parents are perfect for each other. Mary Anne and I have always thought so. So why don't they just get married?"

"I guess it isn't that easy," pointed out Kristy. "Look at how long Mom held off before she agreed to marry Watson. She didn't want to make another mistake. She'd already had one bad marriage."

"*Dad* didn't," said Mary Anne.

"But my mom did," said Dawn. "Maybe it's better that they're waiting."

Just then the phone rang and Corrie's mother called. Mallory arranged a sitting job for me and then asked, "How is Corrie these days?"

I'd written a lot about her in the notebook, so the other girls (I mean, besides Mary Anne) were aware of Corrie and her problems.

"You know, I actually think she's a little better," I replied. "Don't you think so, Mary Anne?"

Mary Anne nodded.

"She still doesn't say much, but I almost take it as a good sign that she seems so attached to me. At least she feels comfortable with *some*body. When we first met, she hardly spoke to anyone at all."

"She barely said two words to me the couple of times I sat for her and Sean," said Dawn. "I'm glad she feels she can talk to you."

I nodded. "It was like something just clicked between us. You know how that happens sometimes? There are people you've known a long time and you know you're never really going to like. And there are people that you meet and *grow* to like. Then there are people you meet and you like instantly. Click! That's pretty much the way it was with Corrie and me."

Mary Anne nodded. "You're right. And it *is* good for her. I mean, to see that it's okay to get close to people, that they're not all going to treat her as casually as her mother does. I just hope she doesn't get too attached to you, Claud."

"If she does, you'll handle it," spoke up Dawn. "Remember when Buddy Barrett got so attached to me? I talked to his mother and everything worked out eventually."

"I hardly ever even *see* Mrs. Addison. She drops Corrie off and picks her up so fast she's just a big blur," I joked.

Dawn smiled.

And Kristy said, "Anyway, we usually do seem to solve our sitting problems. And when we don't, the kids do it themselves. Think of the times *they've* come through. Charlotte Johanssen was pretty attached to Stacey, but when Stacey moved, Charlotte handled it."

"Boy," said Jessi, "I've got a problem I wish *I* could handle. I've heard there are going to be auditions for the ballet *Swan Lake* at the Civic Center — "

"Are you going to try out?" squealed Mal, before Jessi could finish.

"Well, that's the thing. Even if the auditions are open to the public — "

"You're not the public," Mallory interrupted again. "You go to a fancy dance school in Stamford. Stoneybrook's Civic Center — "

" — is pretty important," said Jessi, interrupting Mal this time.

(The rest of us were turning our heads from right to left, left to right, as they spoke.)

"In fact, the productions at the Civic Center," Jessi went on, "are practically off-off-Broadway. Anyway, even if I were allowed to audition, would I really want to? And would my parents let me?"

"Why wouldn't you want to?" I asked.

"Because I'd be competing with professional dancers. Or near-professional dancers, anyway," Jessi replied.

"Don't *you* want to be professional one day?" Mal asked.

"Ye-es . . ."

"Then I think you ought to start competing," I interrupted. "Mimi always said — well, she didn't exactly say it this way, but she said something that meant, 'Give it all you've got.' Otherwise you'll never know what you're culpable of."

"Capable of," Mary Anne corrected me.

"Whatever."

Jessi nodded solemnly, but Mal's face broke into a grin. "Mimi," she said dreamily. "Remember the time she didn't want to go to that county fair with your family, Claud, so she pretended she was sick? Just like a kid who doesn't want to go to school."

"Mm-hmm," I replied shortly. I stared down at the bedspread.

Silence. Dead silence, so to speak. I had brought the discussion to a screeching halt.

After a few moments, Mal said tentatively, "Claudia? I — "

"Be quiet," I said softly. "I don't want to talk about Mimi."

"But on the night before her funeral — " Mal persisted.

"Be *quiet!* I just told you I don't want to talk about her."

"Okay, okay."

"Claud," said Kristy, "this may not be the right time to bring this up, but that never stopped me before." Kristy tried to sound light, but nobody laughed.

"Bring what up?" I said testily. "It better

not have anything to do with Mimi."

"Well, it doesn't . . . exactly."

Even I was disappointed when the phone rang right then. My phone is a blessing and a curse. Sometimes we're saved by it, sometimes it can be *so* inconvenient.

A job was arranged for Kristy, the phone rang twice more, and afternoon jobs were lined up for Jessi and Mal.

Then Kristy picked up where she'd left off. "What I want to say, Claud, is more about Corrie than about Mimi. I know you're filling up a hole in Corrie's life. But I think she's doing the same for you."

After a long pause, I whispered, "Mimi's hole?"

Kristy nodded. "And you have to watch it when you let someone fill a hole. Especially when it's being filled by a kid like Corrie. I don't really believe you'd do this, but just think over what I'm going to say: *Don't drop Corrie.* You're going to start feeling better, Claud, and when you do, you won't need Corrie as much. So don't — don't just drop her."

I was about to protest when Kristy went on, "I don't think you'll do that, though. I think you and Corrie are good for each other and just happen to need each other right now. I think each of you can help the other one get stronger. Be careful, that's all. Everyone says little kids don't break, but they do. Inside. I broke when my father walked out on us."

I gulped and nodded, thinking that I felt pretty broken myself. But I saw Kristy's point and told her so.

Kristy may be a loudmouth. She may be bossy sometimes. But I think she understands kids better than any of the rest of us does.

The meeting ended then, and my friends left club headquarters solemnly.

# CHAPTER 12

A week passed. My grades were dropping.

My grades aren't too good to begin with, but they're pretty stable. Your average C work with an occasional B or D thrown in. I've been known to fail tests.

But when I dropped to a solid D average, no one seemed surprised or even said anything. And that surprised *me*. Ordinarily, my parents would have hit the roof, and my teachers would have called me in for conferences. They'd have said things like, "We know you can do better. You're a smart girl. You have a high I.Q." (That's true. I do.) Or, "We know you can do better. You're Janine's sister." That was the killer. It was also the point. I'm Janine's *sister*, not *Janine*.

Anyway, except for feeling tired all the time, I wasn't sure why my grades had gone down. I did my homework more often than usual. I read all the chapters that were assigned to us. But I'll admit that it was hard to concentrate. Maybe that was because suddenly it had become hard *not* to think about Mimi. For awhile, I tried to shut her out of my mind. Now I couldn't. But why didn't someone say something to me? Why did they let my grades slide? Just because Mimi had died? Mimi would have wanted me to do well in school, if I could.

I was angry at my teachers and my parents.

At least Dorrie and Ashley and my other classmates were speaking to me again. But they wouldn't talk about Mimi, which was funny, because now I wanted to talk about her. Now if Mallory had said, "Remember the time when Mimi . . ." I would have been all ears.

But I did find some sympathy cards slipped into my locker at school, and in our mailbox at home, from my classmates. Mostly, they were flowery cards with printed messages inside that said things like: *I share your sorrow and extend my sympathy.* Or: *What you have once cherished you will never lose.* Or even poems like: *Sometimes words just aren't enough, but I want you to know,* da-da da-da da-da da-da da-da da-da da-doe. (You know what I mean.) And then

Dorrie or Ashley or whoever would sign her name (or his name) under the message.

I guess it's hard to know what to do when someone dies. I tried to think what I would do if, for instance, Kristy's mother or grandmother or someone close to her died. I would talk to her and hug her — if that was what she wanted. But if Dorrie's mother died I would send her a card and sign my name. Maybe it depends on how well you know the person.

Saturday mornings. I looked forward to them thirstily. They were oases in my desert. The kids and their puppets kept me going.

The puppets were almost done.

In fact, on one particular Saturday, everyone was due to finish their puppets during class, except for Marilyn and Carolyn, who had already finished theirs. The other kids were just putting on the last touches, such as hair.

I watched Corrie solemnly glue yellow yarn to the top of Nancy Drew's head. I watched Jamie glue antennae to his space monster. I watched Gabbie just decorate and decorate her doll. I could tell her puppet wouldn't be finished until class was over because she could always think of one more thing to add. She kept exclaiming, "Oh! I'll put these sparkly things on her dress!" Or, "She needs barrettes in her hair. Mary Anne Spier, can you please help me make barrettes?"

Meanwhile, the twins made collages with the materials the other kids were using on their puppets. While they worked, Marilyn announced, "We know a good joke." She was speaking for herself and her sister.

"Yeah," said Carolyn. "And since there are two of us, we can tell it better. See, once there were these two brothers and their names were Trouble and Shut Up. And one day they went downtown to go shopping and Trouble got lost. Shut Up was scared so he went looking for a policeman, and this is what happened. I'm going to play the part of Shut Up and Marilyn will be the policeman."

"I always have to be the policeman," complained Marilyn.

"That's because you're good at it," Carolyn told her.

Marilyn looked like she wanted to protest, but Carolyn said, "Come *on*. Let's finish the joke."

"Okay," agreed Marilyn sulkily.

The rest of the joke went like this:

Carolyn: "Oh, Mr. Policeman! Mr. Police-man!"

Marilyn: "What's the matter, little boy?"

Carolyn, pretending to cry: "I lost my brother and I can't find him."

Marilyn: "What's your name?"

Carolyn: "Shut Up."

Marilyn: "Are you looking for trouble?"

Carolyn: "Yes, I just told you that."

I think there must have been more to the joke, but the twins stopped telling it because the other kids were laughing so hard, and anyway it was time to clean up. As we put things away, I kept hearing Jamie and Myriah giggle and murmur things like, "Are you look-ing for TROUBLE?!!"

Half an hour later the kids and their puppets and collages were gone. Except for Corrie and Nancy Drew. Corrie and I sat on our stoop as usual. Time went by. So much time, in fact, that Mary Anne returned from walking Jamie and the Perkins girls home, and joined us on the stoop.

"What are you going to do with Nancy Drew?" Mary Anne asked Corrie.

Corrie glanced at me and smiled. "Give it to my mom," she replied. "She will be so, so pleased. It will be a special present for her, and she will see that I did well in art. That way, I can make her happy."

"I hope *you* like the puppet, too," said Mary Anne.

"Oh, I do," Corrie told her hastily. "But this is for Mommy. I can show her how much I love her."

At that moment, I heard our front door open behind us.

"Claudia?" It was Janine. "Your phone was ringing upstairs, so I answered it. It's Mrs. Addison. She wants to talk to you."

"Thanks, Janine," I said, glancing at Mary Anne. The two of us exchanged a look that plainly said, "What now?" which I hoped Corrie didn't see. Corrie was probably thinking, What now? herself, though.

Janine stepped outside to sit with Corrie and Mary Anne, and I dashed up to my room. I picked up the receiver, which Janine had placed on the bed.

"Hello? Mrs. Addison?" I said.

"Hi, Claudia. Sorry to do this to you. I'm running late, as you can see."

"Yes. Corrie is waiting for you," I said pointedly.

"Well, the thing is, I've been held up doing

116

my errands." (She did sound like she was calling from a pay phone on the street.) "My bracelet won't be ready at the jewelry store for another half an hour, and the man at the laundry is running late, too." (What a tragedy, I thought.) "So I was wondering if you'd keep Corrie for another hour or so, dear. I'll pay you whatever the rate is for an unexpected call like this."

"Well, I — " I began. Luckily, I was free. But what if I hadn't been? This was pretty pushy of Mrs. Addison. As it was, I'd planned to do some homework that afternoon and finish up a project for my pottery class.

"Oh, that's wonderful," said Mrs. Addison breathily, before I could tell her any of those things. "Tell Corrie I'll be along. Thanks a million. 'Bye!" She hung up.

Oh, brother, I thought. Now I've got to go downstairs and give Corrie this news. I walked slowly to the front door, opened it slowly, and sat down slowly when Corrie, Janine, and Mary Anne squished aside to make room for me.

"Corrie," I said, deciding just to come out and say it, "your mom's running late. She asked me to watch you for another hour or so while she finishes her errands. So why don't you come inside and we'll have some lunch? I don't know about you, but I'm getting hungry. Then I'll show you all the art stuff up in my room."

I just kept talking away as Corrie's face fell. Mary Anne and Janine played along with me nicely, though.

Mary Anne stood up and stretched, as if she heard stories like this every day. Then she said, "I guess I better be going. I'm getting hungry myself. See you next Saturday, Corrie." Then she ran across the street to her house.

And Janine said, "We've got peanut butter and jelly, Corrie. And tunafish, I think. Let's go make sandwiches. Maybe Mom and Dad will let us fix chocolate milk shakes in the blender."

I was surprised. Janine planned to stick with us? Usually she's stuck to her computer. But, I suddenly realized, she hadn't been quite so stuck to it since Mimi had died. She'd spent more time with me. She knew about my stop-action painting, my pottery class, the D I'd gotten on a math quiz, and even where the portrait of Mimi was stashed.

Janine and I rose, and Corrie reluctantly followed us into the house, clutching Nancy

Drew. We made sandwiches and milk shakes, and Mom and Dad knew enough to let the three of us eat alone. People can practically *see* how timid Corrie is.

All during lunch, poor Corrie kept saying things like, "Where's Daddy, I wonder?" and, "Who's watching Sean?" and, "Do you think Mommy will pick up Sean or me first?"

When Mrs. Addison finally did arrive (she honked her car horn from the street more than two hours later), Corrie looked at me tearfully, thanked me for making milk shakes, and handed me Nancy Drew.

"Here. You take her," she said. "I don't want Mommy to have her after all. I want you to have her."

Whoa, I thought as I watched the Addisons drive away. As terrible as I felt about Mimi, I realized one good thing. Mimi was gone, but I'd known her love. I was lucky.

It must, I decided, be awfully difficult to be Corrie Addison.

# CHAPTER 13

After Corrie left, I went to my room and tried to catch up on some of the things I was behind on, and to do over some of the things I'd done poorly in the first place. For most of the afternoon I felt like Mimi was watching me, and that was a good feeling. It was as if she were sitting next to me, patiently helping me, just like she used to do. She would say, "No, look at problem again, my Claudia. Read carefully. Slow down. You can find answer."

Sometimes — not often, but sometimes — she used to climb the steps to the second floor, sit in my room, and watch me work on a painting, a collage, a sculpture, a piece of jewelry. Those times she never said anything. She just watched, and occasionally nodded or smiled. Maybe right now she was thinking about the Muses. Maybe Mimi would become my own personal Muse. Whatever she was, it was nice having her with me. I felt as if she hadn't left us after all.

Our family ate dinner together that night, and I wondered whether the Addisons were doing the same thing, or if Corrie and Sean were eating alone while their parents got dressed to go to a fancy party or something.

When dinner was over, Dad and I cleaned up the kitchen, Mom took the newspaper into the living room, and Janine disappeared, maybe to work on her computer. But those days, who knew? When the kitchen was clean, I left it to go back to my homework. On the way to the stairs, I passed Mimi's bedroom.

The door was open. The light was on. And Janine was sitting on Mimi's bed with the contents of Mimi's jewelry box spilled in front of her.

I was shocked. None of us had been able to go into Mimi's room since the morning she'd died and I'd closed the door.

"We'll give her clothes and things away to charities — to the Salvation Army, maybe — someday soon," Mom kept saying. "Then we'll turn this into a nice guest bedroom."

But no one had opened Mimi's door. We couldn't do it.

Now Janine was in there, pawing through Mimi's most precious things.

She looked up and saw me hovering in the doorway. "Oh, Claudia," she said. "Come here. Look at this pin." She held it out to me. "I think Mimi would want you to have it since she gave me her earrings."

I glanced briefly at the pin. It was a simple circle of pearls set on a ring of gold. It was not my kind of jewelry at all. But that wasn't the point.

"What are you doing in here?" I said with a gasp.

Janine sighed. "I knew you would ask," she replied. "It's time somebody did this. Look. Here's a ring I know Mimi wanted Mom to have. And here's a bar pin. Ooh, I bet Dad could have it made into a tie tack. Wow, look at *this* pin. . . . Oh, I remember this bracelet. Mimi wore it to my eighth-grade graduation."

Janine was holding up one piece of jewelry after another. The clincher was when she found a pair of gold earrings and made a grab for them. "Wow! Here are the flower earrings. I'd forgotten about these. I always wanted them, ever since I was little. They'd look great with my white sweater."

Ha! Who was Janine kidding? She doesn't

care how she looks. Even Kristy pays more attention to what she wears than Janine does.

I exploded. "Oh, my lord, Janine. How could you do this? How *could* you?" I didn't give my sister a chance to answer me. I plowed right ahead. "Mimi's hardly been gone at all and here you are picking through her things like someone with a fine-tooth comb."

"You're mixing your metaphors," said Janine through clenched teeth.

I ignored her. "You're like those awful people in *A Christmas Carol* who wait until Mr. Scrooge is just barely dead and then they go through his room and steal all his stuff, even the rings from his bed curtains, and sell them for practically nothing," I told her.

"I do not," said Janine haughtily, "have plans to sell Mimi's things. I just thought Mimi would want us to have them. Peaches and Russ, too."

"Well, I don't think you should be doing this," I shouted. My voice was getting louder and louder, but I couldn't help it. "Why would anyone want Mimi's dumb old stuff anyway? I hate Mimi. *I hate her!*"

"Hey, hey, what's going on in here?" cried Mom.

She and Dad had appeared behind me in

the hallway. I'm sure, from the way I'd been screaming, that they'd expected to find me murdering Janine. As it was, they were pretty surprised just to see Mimi's room lit up, and my sister on the bed in front of the open jewelry box.

"Nothing," I replied.

Needless to say, my parents didn't believe me.

"Into the living room for a family conference," said Dad.

We gathered in the living room. As we were sitting down, I saw Janine stuff something in the pocket of her skirt.

"All right," my mother began. "Would somebody please explain what was going on?"

Janine told Mom and Dad about the jewelry box, and Mom just looked sort of sad and said that we should have had the courage to go into Mimi's room long ago. I opened my mouth to say something, then closed it again.

After a moment of silence, Dad said gently, "Claudia? Is there anything you'd like to tell us? Your mother and I did hear you say that you hate Mimi. Um . . ."

I could see how uncomfortable he was, so I started talking. "Well," I said, "I didn't realize it at first. I mean, I didn't realize it until right now, but I'm — I'm sort of mad at Mimi." My voice had grown so soft that my family had to lean forward to hear me.

"Why?" asked Mom.

"Because . . ." (I was just figuring this out), "because she left us."

"What do you mean?"

"I mean that she wasn't really sick. She was getting better. She was going to come home from the hospital — and then she died. It's like she just gave up. Like she didn't even care about us enough to stay around awhile longer." There. I'd said it. Even though I hadn't known it, I'd been carrying around that big, bad secret — and I'd finally let it out. No wonder I'd felt so tired lately. Keeping bad secrets takes a lot of energy. "I *tried* not to be mad at Mimi," I assured my parents and sister, remembering how comforted I'd felt that afternoon, feeling that Mimi was near me. "I really tried. Plus, how could I be mad at her when she should have been mad at me?"

Everyone looked puzzled again, so I had to explain about the horrible things I'd done that I felt guilty over. "I bet she thought she was a nuisance," I said. And then with horror I added, "Maybe *that* was why she wanted to die. So she wouldn't have to be a nuisance to us anymore."

"Oh, Claudia!" exclaimed my mother. She jumped up from her armchair, crossed the room, and sat down next to me on the couch, enfolding me in her arms.

"Mimi didn't *want* to die," spoke up Janine softly, and we all looked at her. We watched her pull the something from her pocket that she'd slipped in there earlier. It was a rumpled piece of paper.

"I think she just knew her time had come and that she was *going* to die," Janine went on. "She was trying to accept it and deal with it. Look at this." Janine held the paper out to my mother. "I found this at the bottom of her jewelry box."

I peered over at it, and my father came to look at it, too. Written in Mimi's funny handwriting (she'd had to switch to her left hand after her stroke), was an obituary. Mimi had been writing her own obituary — all the stuff about where she was born and who she was survived by. But the weirdest thing was the date of her death. She'd included that, too, and she'd listed it as this year.

"She knew," I whispered.

126

My mother nodded. "I really don't think she could have held out any longer, Claudia. She might have felt like a nuisance, that's true. But that didn't have anything to do with the timing of her death. She didn't give up, or let herself die. It's like Janine said. She must have known her time had come. And finally her heart just gave out. I think she was sicker than anyone, even the doctors, knew — except Mimi. She knew."

"The doctors *should* have known!" I cried, exploding again. "They should have done more. They're supposed to be trained. They're supposed to be so smart, but they let Mimi die. They never even figured out what was wrong with her. What a bunch of jerks. They should have saved her, but I bet they didn't even try. They probably thought to themselves, 'Oh, she's just an old lady. It doesn't matter.' Well, it matters to me!"

My family listened to my outburst, and I felt better when I was finished. It was a whole lot easier to be mad at the doctors, since I didn't really know them, than it was to be mad at Mimi. And I felt like I had to be mad at someone.

"Claudia," said my father, "can you remember some nice times you had with Mimi, instead of the bad days at the end?"

"Yes," I answered, feeling my throat tighten. I thought of the night before the funeral, sitting around Mary Anne's kitchen table with my friends. "Yes," I repeated.

Mom and Dad and Janine and I talked about Mimi a little longer, and Mom said that, now that the door to Mimi's room was open, we really should clean it out and fix it up. The rest of us agreed. In fact, we left the living room then and went into Mimi's room. Janine plopped herself down on the bed again, Mom and Dad stepped inside and began to look around, and I hovered in the doorway.

"We can't get rid of the things on her walls," I said. "The haiku poem and stuff. I think those should stay here."

My dad agreed. "They'll look very nice in the guest bedroom," he said. "All we need to give away are her personal items. Her clothes and jewelry and things."

Mom hesitated, then opened the door to Mimi's closet. "I'd kind of like to have her kimono," she said.

Dad picked up a paperweight from the table. "I'd like to keep this," he said, turning it over in his hands. Then, "Hey!" he exclaimed. "There's a piece of tape on the bottom with

128

my initials on it. I guess Mimi wanted me to have it, too."

The four of us began looking through everything in Mimi's room. Lots of things were labeled. Mimi had been thinking ahead. We took the items that were marked for us, and set aside those for Russ and Peaches.

"The jewelry isn't marked, though," Janine pointed out, and she held the pearl pin toward me.

This time I took it. I knew I would never wear it, but I would always keep it, because it had belonged to Mimi.

## CHAPTER 14

Another Saturday, another art class.

With the puppets finished, we were trying something more abstract. Collages — even though Marilyn and Carolyn had each made one already. They didn't mind making seconds, though. Their first ones had been made with feathers and sequins, crepe paper and glitter, scraps of felt and lace. Their new ones were going to be made up solely of words and pictures cut from magazines and were to be in the form of birthday cards for their father.

Everyone was hard at work.

Jamie, remembering the twins' joke about Trouble and Shut Up, had decided to invent a joke of his own. "Why," he asked expansively, "did the little girl slide down the slide on her toenail?"

"Why?" asked Gabbie.

"Because she wanted to!" hooted Jamie.

130

He didn't quite have the hang of jokes yet, but most of the kids let out giggles anyway, I guess at the ridiculous thought of someone actually sliding down anything on one toenail.

When the giggling died down, Carolyn leaned over and whispered something to Corrie, who nodded.

A few moments later, Corrie whispered something to Jamie, who also nodded.

What was going on? A secret?

I could understand that. I had a secret of my own. I was working on a special project in my room. I worked on it in between school assignments and assignments for my art classes and my stop-action painting and baby-sitting and club meetings. It was slow-going, as you can imagine, because of everything else I had to do, but that didn't matter. What mattered was that I was working on it. But I didn't tell anyone about it. It was a secret from my family and my friends. I didn't even mention it to Stacey when we talked on the phone. And Stacey knew about everything else — about how the kids at school had acted, about Janine and the jewelry box, and being mad at Mimi and the doctors. But she didn't know my secret.

Soon everyone would, though.

"Claud?" said Mary Anne, interrupting my thoughts.

"Yeah?"

"I hate to say this, but I think we're running out of glue."

That morning, with the help of Corrie, our early bird, Mary Anne and I had filled little paper pill cups with glue, one for each kid. Collages take a lot of glue. Even so, it was hard to believe we were already running out. But I looked around the table, and the children were literally scraping the bottoms of the cups.

"Okay," I said, "I'll go get the big glue bottle."

The big glue bottle, unfortunately, was in my room, so I had to run up two long flights of stairs — from the basement to the first floor, then from the first floor to the second floor — in order to get it.

When I returned with the glue, I got the distinct impression that Mary Anne and the kids had been talking about something, but had stopped as soon as I appeared. More secrets?

Before I could ask, Corrie spoke up shyly. "Claudia?" she began. "Could a collage be a mural, too?"

"What's a mural?" asked Gabbie.

"It's a very big picture," I told her, trying to sign to Matt Braddock at the same time so that he wouldn't be left out of the conversation. "You could make a drawing on a long, long piece of paper. For instance, you could draw a picture of going for a drive. You could show your street, then your town, then the countryside and a farm. Something like that."

"Oh," said Gabbie, and the others, who had been listening intently, nodded.

"But could you make a collage mural?" asked Corrie again.

"Well, I guess so," I answered.

"Goody!" exclaimed several of the children.

"Is that what you'd like to try next?" I asked.

"Yes," replied Myriah firmly.

I was pleased. The kids were learning new art forms and trying to combine them on their own. That was important.

"Can we start next week?" asked Marilyn.

"Sure," I replied.

"We'll need *all* these materials," added Carolyn. "The scraps and glitter and stuff *plus* the magazine pictures and the words."

"You know how you guys could help out?" I said, since I was running out of magazines. "You could each bring in a couple of old magazines and even a newspaper, okay?"

I signed to Matt to make sure he understood what we were doing.

Matt nodded, looking excited.

At that moment, the doorbell rang.

"I'll have to get it," I said to Mary Anne. "Dad's gardening in the backyard, and Mom and Janine are out."

"Okay," agreed Mary Anne. The kids were working busily. Everything was under control.

I dashed up the steps two at a time, ran to our front door, and peered out the side window. Was I ever surprised to see Mrs. Addison standing there! The art class wouldn't be over for another fifteen minutes.

I opened the door. "Hi," I said. (I know I sounded as surprised as I felt.)

"Hi," replied Mrs. Addison. "I'm sorry I'm so early. My husband's waiting in the car." (She turned and gave a little wave toward a blue Camaro parked crookedly in our driveway, as if the Addisons were in a big hurry.) "I forgot to tell Corrie this morning that we have tickets to the ice show in Stamford. I mean, tickets for Sean and Corrie. They'll meet a baby-sitter there, and then Mr. Addison and I can enjoy an afternoon to ourselves."

I could feel my temper rising. An afternoon to themselves? Wasn't that all they *ever* had?

Time without their children? Dumping them at lessons, with friends, with sitters? I counted to five before I said slowly and deliberately something that both Mary Anne and I had been wanting to say to the Addisons for a long time. Mary Anne really should have been the one to say it, since she's better with words than I am. But, oh well. There was Mrs. Addison, and there I was. It might be our only chance.

"Mrs. Addison," I began, trying to think of ways to be tactful, "this is the first time you've picked Corrie up early."

"Yes, I — " she began.

But I kept on talking. "Did you know that Corrie is always the last one to leave my house after class is over? And that she's always the first to arrive?"

Mrs. Addison checked her watch impatiently and glanced over her shoulder at the car waiting in our driveway.

"I love having Corrie around," I went on. "She's a terrific kid. But, well, she feels pretty bad about being left here . . . left here longer than any of the other children, I mean."

Mrs. Addison's expression changed. She looked at me curiously.

"Did you notice," I started to ask, "that Corrie hasn't brought home any of her art projects?"

"Well," (Mrs. Addison cleared her throat), "I noticed that just, um, just this morning. And I did wonder why."

"It's because she's been giving them away," I said.

"Giving them away?"

I nodded. "Yes. To me, to Mary Anne Spier, to the other kids. I think," I began (and oh, my lord, I hoped I wasn't butting in where I didn't belong), "that Corrie is a little bit mad at you and Mr. Addison." (What an understatement.) "She wants to please you, but she gets angry and scared when she feels like," (I tried to think of a nice way to say that Corrie felt her parents didn't care about her), "like . . . sometimes other things are more important to you and Mr. Addison than she is."

There. I'd said it. I waited for the fireworks.

But Mrs. Addison merely looked at me with tears in her eyes. She rummaged around in her purse for some Kleenex.

"All Corrie wants," I dared to say, "is to spend more time with you."

Mrs. Addison began to sniffle. "Excuse me," she said hurriedly, and ran out the door and back to her car.

Uh-oh, I thought. Now I've done it. I stood at the door on rubbery legs. A few minutes later, Mrs. Addison returned. I was still at the door.

"I think," Mrs. Addison began, "that the baby-sitter probably wouldn't mind if I attended the ice show with Sean and Corrie today. I can pass up my free afternoon."

"You can?!" I grinned. And you should have seen the look on Corrie's face when her mother and father not only gave Corrie the news about the ice show, but took a tour of our makeshift art room. Corrie even presented her parents with her newly finished collage.

"This is for you," she said proudly, hastily scrawling

*Love, Corrie*

across the back.

A few moments later, the Addisons and Corrie climbed the basement steps.

I watched them go. I knew that Corrie's life wouldn't magically change, that it wouldn't be perfect from then on. But I thought maybe it would be better. And I realized that Mimi was the one who had shown me how it *could* be better. Because Mimi had always been there when I needed her. I never had to fight for her love the way Corrie had to fight for her parents' love. Now Mimi might be gone, but I knew that before she died (*died*, not *left me*), she had made me a strong person, strong enough to stand up to Mrs. Addison for Corrie.

# CHAPTER 15

I will now reveal my secret.

My secret was a tribute to Mimi. It was a piece of art. Mimi had always appreciated my art. She liked anything I did, but she especially liked my paintings and collages. And so, since the kids and I seemed to have collage fever, I made a collage for Mimi.

It was not very big — only about twelve inches by twelve inches, and I filled it with small but important things. Maybe I did that because Mimi had always seemed small but important to me. She was tiny — birdlike — but she could help me to solve any problem or make me feel better even when I was at my lowest of lows.

So the collage contained small pictures cut from magazines — of a tea cup and saucer to represent our "special tea"; of a family eating a meal, since Mimi had always cooked for us and insisted that we eat together; and of a woman knitting, since Mimi liked to do needlework before she had her stroke. Then I drew a picture of a Japanese woman cradling a Japanese baby. I added that, too, plus yarn and ribbon, thread and lace. I even glued down tiny charms — scissors and a thimble — and tea leaves and flour.

I hoped the collage was impressive and meaningful, but I wasn't sure. Even so, I backed it, matted it, and had it framed. That cost a lot of baby-sitting money, but I didn't care. It was for Mimi.

And now it was time to unveil it. As far as I knew, nobody had any idea about my secret. I decided to show it to my friends first, then my family. If my friends didn't like it, or thought it was stupid, they would tell me so. I could count on them for that. Then I could change it, or start over, before I showed it to my family. I wanted my family to see the polished, perfect tribute, not something silly or full of mistakes.

So at the next meeting of the Baby-sitters Club, when we were gathered in my room and Kristy said, "Any club business?" I raised my hand tentatively.

Kristy looked at me curiously. Mallory and

Jessi are usually the only ones who bother to raise their hands. In fact, Kristy has never asked us to do that. It's just that Mal and Jessi are younger, and the sixth-grade teachers still drill that stuff about hand-raising into your head at their age. By eighth grade, the teachers have pretty much given up.

"Claud?" said Kristy.

"I — I know this isn't club, um, club business," I stammered, "so if you don't want to hear about it right — right now, that's okay . . . I guess. I mean, this is Mimi business, and you all knew her, and you know how im — important she was to me." (To my horror, I could feel tears welling up in my eyes.) "I want to — to show you something."

I could feel every single person in my room, even Kristy, melting.

And Kristy was the one to say, "Of course we want to see . . . whatever it is. Don't we, you guys?"

The others agreed without hesitating.

I drew in a deep breath, then let it out slowly. "Okay," I began, "what it is, is a tribute to Mimi. I wanted to do something in her memory. *Having* memories is one thing, but I wanted to do something *for* her. Even though she's not — not here, I think she'll know I did

141

it. I know that sounds weird, but I really feel it's true."

I eased myself off the bed, where I'd been sandwiched between Dawn and Mary Anne, crossed the room to my closet, and emerged with the collage. I set it on the bed, and my friends crowded around for a look.

At first nobody said a word, and a cold feeling washed over me. "It's terrible, isn't it?" I said. "It's really dumb."

"Oh, no," breathed Dawn. "It's perfect. It — it says Mimi all over. I mean, it *is* Mimi. It's Mimi the way we want to remember her."

"Yeah," said Kristy, Jessi, and Mal.

And Mary Anne burst into tears. I think that was what finally convinced me that the collage was all right, not all wrong, that I'd done my job. The collage really was a tribute. In Dawn's words, it said Mimi all over.

I decided I could show it to my parents and Janine. And I decided to do so that night after dinner.

I waited until the kitchen had been cleaned up and everyone was about to begin their evening activities. Janine was heading upstairs to her computer, Mom was sitting down at the desk in the living room to pay bills, and Dad was just opening the paper.

"You guys?" I said.

My parents and sister turned toward me.

"I have something to show you." Even though my friends had honestly loved the collage, I began to feel nervous again.

"What is it, sweetie?" asked Mom.

"It's something for Mimi," I replied. "And something for us to remember her by. I'll go get it." I ran to my room, retrieved the collage from my closet, and brought it back downstairs. Then I stood before my family with the front of the collage pressed against my chest.

"Well," I said, "um, this is it." I turned it around.

"Why, Claudia, it's *perfect!*" exclaimed my mother, stepping forward for a closer look.

Dad and Janine peered at it, too, and it was Janine who glanced at the fireplace and said, "I think we should hang it over the mantelpiece."

"That's a wonderful idea," agreed Dad.

But I said, "Thanks. Thank you, guys, for wanting to put it in the living room, but I had a different idea. I mean, if you don't mind, I was wondering if we could put the collage in Mimi's room. I know it's going to become our guest room, but it's been Mimi's room for as long as I can remember, and I like leaving the — the flavor of Mimi there."

"Well, of course you can," said Mom and Dad at the same time. (If they'd been any younger they would have had to hook pinkies and say "jinx.")

And so we hung the collage in Mimi's room. We put it right over her (empty) dresser. Then the four of us stood back and looked at it, feeling quite pleased.

"Mimi would have loved it," said Dad.

The next Saturday was art-class day, of course, and two unusual things happened. First of all, Corrie arrived on time, not early. In fact, Myriah and Gabbie were already in the basement by the time Mrs. Addison dropped Corrie off.

Second, when all the children had arrived, Mary Anne announced, "Claudia, today you are not allowed in the basement."

"But I'm the teacher," I protested, surprised.

"And I'm second-in-command," Mary Anne countered, "and the kids are third-in-command. And we say, 'Out.' Today you are on vacation because we're working on something special and secret."

Ah-*ha!* A secret. I knew it.

144

"Go upstairs and work on your painting or something."

So I did, all the time wondering just what was going on in the basement. I wasn't worried, with Mary Anne in charge, but I was awfully curious.

Just before class was over, Mary Anne called me back down to the basement. I practically flew there. When I hit the bottom step I was greeted by two things: the sound of Jamie, Marilyn, Carolyn, Corrie, Myriah, Gabbie, and Mary Anne shouting, "Surprise!" (while Matt signed to me), and the sight of the kids' mural-collage.

"It's for Mimi! It's for Mimi!" cried Jamie, jumping up and down.

Mary Anne smiled at me. "The kids thought this up on their own. They didn't know a thing about *your* collage for Mimi. They started talking about this two weeks ago. They wanted to do something for Mimi, just like you did."

I leaned over the table to get a good look at the collage. It didn't really have much to do with Mimi herself, and it was kind of messy — blobs of glue here and there, cotton balls hanging by threads, fingerprints, drippy paint, but the kids were terribly proud of it.

"I'll tell you what we're going to do with

145

it," I said, after I had thanked everyone about a million times. "We're going to put it in Mimi's room, where it belongs. But it's so big I'll have to wait until Dad can help me."

That was okay with the kids. It was time to leave anyway. Just as the doorbell started ringing with arriving parents, Corrie tugged at my arm and pulled me to a corner of the basement, away from the others.

"*I* made something for *you*," she said. "Something special. Mimi deserved a — a what do you call it?"

"A tribute?" I suggested.

"Yes, a tribute. And so do you. So this is for you."

Corrie thrust something at me that she'd been hiding behind her back.

I took it carefully. It was a sketch, and I could tell it was a sketch of me. It was very good.

"Thank you, Corrie," I whispered, kneeling down to give her a hug.

"Mrs. Addison's here!" Janine called just then from upstairs.

"Right on time," said Corrie with a grin.

I grinned back. It was nice to know I'd made a difference in Corrie's life. It was even nicer

146

to know who had helped me to make that difference.

Mimi.

As soon as the basement was cleaned up and everyone had gone, there was something I would have to do. So I did it just after the last kid had been ushered out the door.

I climbed the stairs slowly to the second floor and opened the door to the attic. I turned on the light.

My portrait of Mimi was leaning against an old filing cabinet where I'd left it the morning she had died. Now I picked it up, brought it into my room, and hung it in its old spot.

I stood back to look at it.

I couldn't say anything to it because of the big lump in my throat.

I just let Mimi smile down at me. After a few moments, I smiled back.

## About the Author

ANN M. MARTIN did *a lot* of baby-sitting when she was growing up in Princeton, New Jersey. Now her favorite baby-sitting charge is her cat, Mouse, who lives with her in her Manhattan apartment.

Ann Martin's Apple Paperbacks are *Bummer Summer, Inside Out, Stage Fright, Me and Katie (the Pest)*, and all the other books in the Baby-sitters Club series.

She is a former editor of books for children, and was graduated from Smith College. She likes ice cream, the beach, and *I Love Lucy*; and she hates to cook.

Look for #27

## JESSI AND THE SUPERBRAT

*P.S. 162* faded off for a commercial break and an ad for some gasoline company came on.

Becca stared dreamily at the TV screen.

"Isn't Lamont just the cutest thing in the world?" she sighed.

"I think Waldo's funnier," I said.

"You like *Waldo?*" Becca said. "So does everyone in my class. Charlotte Johanssen said that the kid who plays him used to go to Stoneybrook Elementary School." (Charlotte Johanssen is Becca's best friend. She's lived in Stoneybrook a lot longer than we have.)

"Is that true?" asked Mama.

"Cross my heart," said Becca. She traced an X on her chest over her heart. I still didn't know whether to believe her. "Charlotte said that he used to always get his picture in the paper here."

Hmm. Well, maybe Becca *was* telling the truth. She certainly seemed to have enough details.

When the show was over I ran to the telephone to call Mallory. I figured if there was any one family that would know about this Waldo business it would have to be the Pikes.

Mallory confirmed everything Becca had said. Waldo and his family *did* live in Stoneybrook. She said that Waldo's real name was Derek Masters, and she told me that before he got the job on the TV show, he had lived here permanently. Now, of course, he had to be out in California for a chunk of the year, so the whole family had moved with him out to L.A. while he was taping *P.S. 162.*

"How do you know all this?" I asked.

"*A star* from *Stoneybrook?* Are you kidding? It's big news. Everybody knows it," said Mallory. "Anyway, Derek used to be in Nicky's class." Nicky is one of Mallory's younger brothers. He's eight years old and in third grade.

"Wow!" I said. I couldn't believe that no one had told me any of this before. This was hot news, and I wanted a chance to talk about it with my friends. I couldn't wait for the next meeting of the Baby-sitters Club.

150

# WIN A VISIT FROM ANN M. MARTIN!

**Enter** THE BABY-SITTERS CLUB® **Super Trivia Contest!**

Which baby-sitter is Ann M. Martin's favorite? Where does she get her ideas?
Get the answers to these questions and more when Ann visits your hometown
and takes you and three of your friends to dinner! One lucky fan will win! Just
correctly answer the questions on the coupon, and mail it by November 30, 1989.

- **2nd prize**–25 Baby-sitters Club T-shirts!
- **3rd prize**–50 pairs of Baby-sitters Club socks!

1. Monday is Dues Day for The Baby-sitters Club. — True or False

2. The Baby-sitters' favorite charge is Jenny Prezzioso. — True or False

3. There are two associate members of The Baby-sitters Club,
   Logan and Karen. — True or False

4. Claudia has a secret admirer on the cruise to Disney World. — True or False

**Rules:** Entries must be postmarked by November 30, 1989. Winners will be picked at random from all eligible
entries received. No purchase necessary. Valid only in the U.S.A. Employees of Scholastic Inc., affiliates,
subsidiaries, and their families not eligible. Void where prohibited. Winners will be notified by mail.

Fill in the coupon below and answer all questions. Mail to: THE BABY-SITTERS CLUB SUPER TRIVIA CONTEST,
Scholastic Inc., P.O. Box 7500, 2931 E. McCarty Street, Jefferson City, MO 65102.

## JOIN THE NEW BABY-SITTERS FAN CLUB!

Every Baby-sitters Fan Club member will receive: a two-year membership; an
official membership card; a colorful banner; and a semi-annual newsletter with
baby-sitting tips, activities and more...all for just $2.50!

*No Purchase Necessary*

## The Baby-sitters Club Super Trivia Contest

Fill in your answers here. Indicate T for True; F for False.

1. _____     2. _____     3. _____     4. _____

Name _____ Age _____

Street _____

City, State, Zip _____

**Where did you buy this Baby-sitters Club book?**

- ☐ Bookstore        ☐ Drug Store
- ☐ Discount Store   ☐ Book Club
- ☐ Supermarket      ☐ Book Fair
- ☐ Other_____
            specify

☐ **Yes!** Enroll me in The Baby-sitters Fan Club! I've enclosed my check or money order
(no cash please) for $2.50 made payable to Scholastic Inc. at the address above.

BSC189

# America's Favorite Series

# THE BABY-SITTERS CLUB®

### by Ann M. Martin

*Collect Them All!*

The seven girls at Stoneybrook Middle School get into all kinds of adventures...with school, boys, and, of course, baby-sitting!

### Available wherever you buy books...or use the coupon below.

Scholastic Inc. P.O. Box 7502, 2932 E. McCarty Street, Jefferson City, MO 65102

Please send me the books I have checked above. I am enclosing $_____

(please add $1.00 to cover shipping and handling). Send check or money order–no cash or C.O.D.'s please.

Name_____

Address_____

City_____ State/Zip_____

Please allow four to six weeks for delivery. Offer good in U.S.A. only. Sorry, mail order not available to residents of Canada.   Prices subject to change.

BSC 289